PRAISE FOR THE HOT NEW TV SERIES
THE X-FILES

"**THE X-FILES** is a rip-roaring hour of TV: suspenseful, scary, fun, imaginative, entertaining, and weird, wonderfully weird."

—Jeff Jarvis
TV Guide

"**THE X-FILES** is undeniably x-tra smart."

—Matt Roush
USA Today

"**THE X-FILES** is a true masterpiece. There's no more challenging series on television and, as a bonus, it's also brainy fun."

—Howard Rosenberg
Los Angeles Times

THE (X)-FILES

GOBLINS

Charles Grant

Based on the characters created
by Chris Carter

HarperPrism
An Imprint of HarperPaperbacks

HarperPaperbacks   *A Division of* HarperCollins*Publishers*
                    10 East 53rd Street, New York, N.Y. 10022

First printing: December 1994

Printed in the United States of America

HarperPrism is an imprint of HarperPaperbacks.
HarperPaperbacks, HarperPrism, and colophon are trade-
marks of HarperCollins*Publishers*

❖ 1 0 9 8 7 6 5

This is for Chris Carter, no question about it.

Because, quite literally, without his wonderful
and addictive show, this book wouldn't exist,
and I wouldn't have anything to do on
Friday nights but work.

ACKNOWLEDGMENTS

Many, many thanks, for reasons that would probably bore you to tears, to:

John Silbersack, editor and keeper of the editorial whip, for extreme patience under fire, and helping me keep mine;

Howard Morhaim, fastest and best damn agent in the West;

The Jersey Conspiracy, whose enthusiastic support kept me sane, and whose invaluable assistance steered me away from making too many stupid mistakes—it isn't their fault if I made them anyway;

T. Liam McDonald, for the inside scoop;

Ms. Carolee Nisbet, Public Affairs Office, Fort Dix, New Jersey, who was always gracious and helpful, especially when blathered memories of basic training kept getting in the way of intelligent discussion—if you don't recognize some of the post as described here, the changes were made for story reasons only, not because Ms. Nisbet steered me wrong.

And last, but never least, to Ashley McConnell, who called one night and ordered me to watch the show, sent me information I couldn't do without, and still hasn't said, "I told you so." Yet.

ONE

The tavern was filled with ghosts that night.

Grady Pierce could feel them, but he didn't much care as long as the bartender kept pouring the drinks.

They were ghosts of the old days, when recruits, mostly draftees, were bused almost daily into Fort Dix for basic training, scared or strutting, and hustled out of their seats by drill instructors with hard faces and hard eyes who never spoke in less than a yell. The scared became terrified, and the strutters soon lost that smug look they wore—it was apparent from the moment they were shorn of their hair that this wasn't going to be a Technicolor, wide-screen John Wayne movie.

This was real.

This was the real Army.

And there was a damn good chance they were going someplace to die.

Grady ought to know; he had trained enough of them himself.

But that was the old days.

This was now, and what the hell—if the ghosts of the boys who never came back wanted to stand behind him and demand he teach them again and this time do it right, well, hell, that was what they did, no skin off his nose.

What he did these days was drink, and damned good at it he was.

He sat on his stool, bony shoulders hunched, hands clasped on the bar before him as if he were saying grace before taking up the glass. His face under the mostly gray brush cut was all angles, sharp and dark with shadows; he wore worn and stained fatigues loose at the waist, a too-large field jacket torn at one shoulder, scuffed hiking boots so thin he could feel pebbles beneath the soles.

From where he sat at the bar's far end, he could see the dozen scarred darkwood tables, the half-dozen dark booths along the side wall, the twenty or so customers bent over their drinks. Usually the place was close to bedlam with top-of-the-voice, not always good-natured arguments about the Giants, the Phillies, the 76ers, the government. Waylon would be howling on the jukebox, a game on the TV hanging on the wall, and beneath it all the comforting clatter of balls over at the pool table, floating green in the light of the single lamp above it. There might even be a few working girls hanging out, joining in, not always looking for business.

Good thing, too, he thought with a quick grin; most of the gals these days were a little long in the tooth and short in the looks.

Tonight, however, was pretty damn miserable.

Rain all day, changing to a hard mist at sundown. The temperature had risen, too, slipping pockets of shifting fog into the alleys and gutters.

It was April, nearly May, but it felt a whole lot like November.

He glanced at his watch—just a few minutes past midnight—and rubbed his eyes with bony knuckles. Time he was having one for the road, then getting on that road while he could still find it.

He reached for the glass, one ice cube and Jack Daniel's halfway to the rim. He frowned and pulled his hand back. He could have sworn that that glass had been full a second ago.

Man, I'm worse than I thought.

He reached for it again.

"You sure about that?" Aaron Noel, who was more muscle than any man had a right to own and still be able to move, flipped a drying towel over his shoulder and leaned back against the shelf fronting the smoke-fogged mirror. His white T-shirt was tight, the sleeves cut off to give his upper arms some room. He was a younger man who looked as if he had lived one lifetime too many. "Not that I'm complaining, Grady, but I ain't taking you home tonight again, no offense."

Grady grinned. "You my old lady now?"

"Nope. But the weather sucks, right? And every time the weather sucks, you get the miseries, drink too much and pass out, and then I gotta lug your sorry ass to that sorry hole you call a house." He shook his head. "No way. Not tonight." He waggled his eyebrows. "Got a meeting when I'm done."

Grady glanced at the window by the exit. Past the neon he could see the mist, the dark street, the empty storefronts on the other side.

"So?" the bartender said, nodding toward the unfinished glass.

Grady straightened, yanked on an earlobe and pinched his cheeks. It was an old trick to see if he was numb enough yet to go home and sleep without having those damn dreams. He wasn't, but he wasn't drunk enough to defy a man who could break his back with his pinky, either.

If the truth be known, Noel was good for him. More than once over the past fifteen years, he had stopped Grady from getting into fights that would have easily turned him into one of his own ghosts. He didn't know why the guy cared; it had just turned out that way.

He considered the glass carefully, grimaced at the way his stomach lurched with acid, and said with a resigned sigh, "Ah, the hell with it."

Aaron approved.

Grady slipped off the stool and held onto the bar with his left hand while he waited for his balance to get it right. When he figured he could walk without looking like he was on a steamer in a hurricane, he saluted the bartender and dropped a bill beside the glass. "Catch you around," he said.

"Whatever," the bartender said. "Just get the hell home and get some sleep."

Grady reached into his hip pocket and pulled out a Yankees cap, snapped it open and jammed it onto his head, and made his way toward the door.

When he checked over his shoulder, Aaron was already talking with another guy at the bar.

"Good night, gentlemen," he said loudly, and stepped outside, laughing at the way some of them snapped their heads up, eyes wide, as if he'd just shaken them out of a nap.

As soon as the door closed behind him, the laughter twisted into a spasm of coughing, forcing him to lean against the brick wall until it passed.

"Jesus," he muttered, wiping his mouth with the back of a hand. "Quit drinking, quit smoking, you old fart, before they find you in the damn gutter."

He paused at the curb, then crossed over and moved on up the street, keeping close to the closed shops, the empty shops with plywood for windows, and decided as he did that he'd finally had it with this burg. As the government kept chipping away at Dix's assignments, folks up and left, and nobody came in to take their place.

Hell, if he was going to drink himself to death, he might as well do it somewhere pretty, Florida or something, where at least it stays warm most of the damn year.

He hiccuped, spat on the sidewalk, and belched loudly.

On the other hand, he decided the same thing every damn night, and hadn't moved yet.

Goddamn Army.

Too old, pal, we don't need you anymore. Take your pension and split, you old fart.

He belched again, spat again, and seriously considered going back to Barney's, to have a farewell drink. That would shake them up, no question about it.

Half a block later he stopped, scowling at himself, and squinted down the street. The tarmac was a black mirror, streetlight and neon twisted and shimmering in the puddles. Nothing there but small shops and offices, a distant traffic light winking amber.

He looked behind him.

The street was deserted there, too.

Nothing moved but small patches of fog.

You're spooking yourself, bud; knock it off.

He rolled his shoulders, straightened his spine, and crossed to the other side. Two more blocks, a left, a right, and he'd be at the worn-down apartment complex where he had spent most of the years since his discharge.

He could find the damn thing blindfolded.

He glanced back again, thinking someone from the bar was following him.

The end of the block, and he turned around.

Damnit, there was someone back there. It wasn't so much the sound of footsteps as it was a presence. A feeling. The certainty that he wasn't alone. He knew that feeling well—it had almost driven him around the bend, over there in the jungle, knowing they were in the trees, watching, waiting, fingers on triggers.

"Hey!" he called, glad for the sound of his voice, wishing it didn't echo so much.

Nothing there.

Yes, there was.

Screw it, he thought, turning with a disgusted wave of his hand; I don't need the aggravation.

If it was another drunk, he didn't care; if it was some kid looking for a quick mugging, he didn't care about that either because he didn't have anything worth taking.

But by the end of the block he couldn't help it; he had to look.

Nothing.

Nothing at all.

A sudden breeze made him narrow his eyes as it sifted mist against his face, and when he did, he saw something move at the mouth of a narrow alley about thirty feet back.

"Hey, damnit!"

No one answered.

And that pissed him off.

Bad enough the Army had fucked him over, and bad enough he hadn't been able to leave this damn place and leave the ghosts behind, but he was not about to let some goddamn punk mess with his head.

He pulled his hands out of his pockets and marched back, breathing slowly, deeply, letting his anger build by degrees instead of exploding.

"Hey, you son of a bitch!"

No one answered.

Nothing moved.

By the time he reached the alley, he was in full-bore fighting mode, and he stood at the mouth, feet slightly apart, fists on his hips.

"You want to come outta there, buddy?"

A sigh; maybe the breeze, maybe not.

He couldn't see more than five feet in—three stories of brick on either side, a pair of dented trash cans on the left, scraps of paper on the ground, fluttering weakly as the breeze blew again.

He wasn't sure, but he thought the alley was a dead end, which meant the sucker wasn't going anywhere as long as he stood here. The question was, how far was he going to push this thing? How drunk was he?

He took one step in, and heard the breathing.

Slow, measured; someone was trying very hard not to be heard.

This didn't make sense. If whoever it was had hidden himself back there, Grady would have heard him moving around. Had to. There was too much crap on the ground, too much water. His own single step had sounded like a gunshot.

And the breathing sounded close.

"I ain't got time for this," he muttered, and turned.

And saw the arm reach out of the brick wall on his right.

The arm, and the hand with the blade.

He knew what it was; God knows he had used it himself dozens of times.

He also knew how sharp it was.

He almost didn't feel it sweep across his throat.

And he almost managed to make it to the street before his knees gave out and he fell against the wall, staring at the arm, at the hand, at the bayonet as he slid down, legs stretched out before him.

"Goddamn ghost," he whispered.

"Not quite," someone answered. "Not quite, old man."

That's when Grady felt the fire around his neck, and the warmth flowing over his chest, and the garbage beneath him, and the fog settling on his face.

That's when he saw the face of the thing that had killed him.

TWO

The afternoon was pleasantly warm, the sky a sharp and cloudless blue. The sounds of Thursday traffic were muted by the trees carrying their new leaves, although the cherry trees hadn't yet sprung all their blossoms. The tourists were few at the Jefferson Memorial, mostly older people with cameras around their necks or camcorders in their hands, moving slowly, taking their time. A handful of joggers followed the Tidal Basin rim; two paddle boats glided over the water, seemingly in a clumsy, not very earnest race.

That's why Fox Mulder preferred this place over the others when he wanted time to think. He could sit undisturbed on the steps, off to one side, without having to listen to terminally bored tour guides chattering like robots, or schoolkids laughing and horsing around, or any of the rest of the circus that Old Abe or the Washington Monument managed to attract.

His dark blue suit jacket was folded on the marble step beside him. His tie was pulled down and his collar unbuttoned. He looked much younger than his years, his face as yet unlined, his brown hair unruly in the light breeze that slipped over the water. Those who bothered to look in his direction figured, he supposed, that he was some kind of academic.

That was all right with him.

His sandwich was almost done, a plastic cup of soda just about empty, when he saw a tall man in a dark brown suit moving around the edge of the Basin, staring at those he passed as if expecting to discover someone he knew. Mulder looked quickly from side to side, but there was no way he could duck around the building or into the trees without being seen.

"Hey!" the man called, catching sight of him and waving.

Mulder smiled politely, but he didn't stand.

This was not what he needed on a great day like this. What he needed was his sandwich, his soda—although he'd prefer a cold beer in a bottle, preferably sitting in a booth at Ripley's, in Alexandria—and maybe that short brunette over there, taking slow tight circles on a pair of in-line skates, earphones attached to a Walkman at her waist. He supposed maintaining balance was a lot like being on ice skates; it seemed to be the same principle. Not that he was all that good when roller skates had wheels at the corners, spending, as he had done, more time on his rump than attaining great speeds.

The skater shifted suddenly, and he blinked, realizing for the first time how tan she was, and how snug her red satin shorts and red T-shirt were.

Then a shadow blocked his view.

It was the redhead.

"Mulder," the man said, standing two steps below him, grinning like an idiot, "where the hell have you been?"

"Right here, Hank."

Special Agent Hank Webber stared over Mulder's head at the daylit figure of Thomas Jefferson standing tall beneath the dome. A puzzled frown came and went. "Never did see this place, you know what I mean?" He shook his head, scratched through his dark red hair. "What do you want to come to a place like this for?"

Mulder shrugged. "It's nice. It's quiet." He deepened his voice. "It's not the office."

Webber didn't take the hint. "So, did you hear what came in?"

Mulder just looked at him.

"Oh." The younger man grinned sheepishly. "Sorry. Of course you wouldn't hear. You were here."

"Hank, your powers of deduction have never failed to give me a shiver." He smiled when the younger man sputtered, telling him with a gesture that it was only a stupid joke. Hank was a good man, but there were times when Mulder thought him dense as a post. "Hear what?"

"Helevito."

He sat up slowly, lunch momentarily forgotten. "What about him?"

"They got him." .

He didn't know whether to laugh, cheer, shock the kid with a victory dance, or play it the Bureau way by simply nodding, as if the outcome of a three-month manhunt for a kidnapper had never been in doubt, especially since the kidnapped child had already been recovered safely. What he decided to do was take another bite of his sandwich.

Webber hooked a thumb in his belt. "Yep. Not two hours ago. You figured it right, Mulder. They staked out his cousin's place in Biloxi, and sure enough, he comes strolling in this morning all by his lonesome. Spent most of the night on one of those new riverboats, pissing away half the ransom money at roulette. Most of the rest evidently went to some blonde." He laughed and shook his head. "I heard the first thing he said was, 'I knew I should've played thirty-six and red.'"

He nodded.

Mulder took another bite, another sip, and waited.

"So." Webber squinted as he checked out the memorial again.

A quartet of nuns chattered past, smiling at him, smiling at Mulder.

The skater left, not even a glance in their direction.

Webber sniffed, and fussed with his tie. "So."

"Hank, I am eating my lunch. I am enjoying the fresh air, the sunshine . . . and I am especially enjoying the peace and quiet that comes with not being at the Bureau for a while. I'm not sure what you want me to say."

The younger man seemed bewildered. "But . . . but if it hadn't been for you, they never would've gotten him, right? I mean, nobody else figured out his gambling problem, right? Nobody else knew about that cousin. So . . ." He spread his hands. "So aren't you glad?"

"Overjoyed," he answered flatly.

And instantly regretted it when Webber's expression sagged into youthful disappointment. He knew the kid believed that every bust was righteous, every arrest an occasion for celebration, every crook large or small put behind bars a reason to dance. What he hadn't figured on was, between the first bust and the fourth and the fiftieth and the millionth, the exhilaration was always there. Always. And the feeling that finally one of the bad guys lost.

But the good agents, the best ones, never forgot that on the far side of that exhilaration there was always someone else waiting in line.

It never ended.

It just never ended.

That fact alone sometimes turned a perfectly good agent into a cynic who made mistakes. And it sometimes got him killed.

Mulder didn't want that to happen to him.

He had too much to do.

He had too much yet left undone.

On the other hand, he also hadn't finished his lunch, and there were still five other folders waiting on his desk in varying stages of investigation. He wasn't the primary agent on any of them, but he had been asked to take a look, to see if he could spot something the others had missed.

It was what he was good at; very good, if you paid attention to some of the talk around the office. Although he really didn't see it that way. It was, simply, what he did, and he had never really bothered to analyze it.

When the younger man finally looked as if he were either going to cry or scream, Mulder swallowed, touched his chin with a finger, and pointed. "If I remember, Hank, you were the one who came up with the Biloxi connection. We all missed it. You got it."

Webber blushed.

He couldn't believe it—the kid actually blushed, ducked his head, scuffed his shoe on the step. Mulder decided that if he said, "Aw, shucks," he would have to be killed.

"Thanks," he said instead, fighting hard not

to grin. "That . . . well, that means a lot." He gestured vaguely. "I didn't mean to interrupt but . . ." He gestured again. "I thought you'd want to know."

"I did. Honestly. Thanks."

"So." Webber backed away, and almost toppled off the step. He laughed self-consciously, his right arm flapping. "So, I guess I'll get back, okay?"

"Sure."

"You'll be—"

Mulder held up what was left of the sandwich.

"Right. Sure." He waved, reached into his jacket pocket, pulled out a pair of sunglasses, and slipped them on.

Suddenly he wasn't a kid named Hank Webber anymore.

Suddenly he was a man in a suit too dark for the weather, wearing sunglasses too dark for the sun. Suddenly he wasn't a part of the scene anymore. If he had painted a sign on his back, he couldn't have said FBI any better.

Mulder smiled to himself as Webber walked off, practically marching, and washed the last of his lunch down with the soda. Then he glanced around, not really seeing anything, before hooking his jacket with a forefinger, draping it over his shoulder, and moving into the memorial itself.

He liked it in here, especially now, when there was no one else around. It didn't feel like a cathedral, the way Old Abe's place did, yet he was in awe just the same of the man who rose above him. Jefferson wasn't a god. He had his faults. But those faults only made his accomplishments all the more remarkable.

This was where he liked to work puzzles out, following crooked mental paths to see where they led, maybe hoping some of the third president's genius would rub off on him.

In here he couldn't hear the traffic, the tourists, nothing but the sound of his shoes on the polished marble floor.

What he had to consider today was a case in Louisiana that involved at least one brutal murder, one daylight robbery of $25,000, and witnesses who swore on every Bible handed to them that the person who had done it had vanished into thin air. In the middle of a circus tent. While wearing the costume of a hobo clown.

His instincts were usually pretty reliable. This time they suggested this had nothing to do with an X-File, those cases he specialized in, that had about them an air of the bizarre, the inexplicable.

The paranormal.

The kind of cases the Bureau officially frowned upon, but couldn't always ignore.

Which was why he had been shown this one. This kind of thing, whether the upper echelon liked it or not—and they usually didn't—was his specialty.

Louisiana just didn't have that X-File scent.

Still, there was always a chance he was wrong. It wouldn't be the first time. His usual partner, Dana Scully, had told him that so often, he had finally suggested she print up cards: *Mulder, this is an ordinary case, only with weird stuff; aliens, monsters, and UFOs need not apply.* Whenever he began to think that X the unknown was actually something they should look into, she was supposed to hand him a card, or staple it to his forehead, and get on with it.

She hadn't thought that very funny.

Except for the stapling part.

Still, he had been right often enough in the past, even if she was too stubborn to admit it.

What he was afraid of now, what always kept him alert, was that every case with supposed "weird stuff" in it would make him jump before he thought, and thus bring down the wrath of his superiors, forcing the X-File Section closed.

It had already happened once.

He didn't want it to happen again.

Especially when he had been so close to final proof that the Earth wasn't alone . . . so close . . .

Too close for some.

Others would call that paranoia; he called it simply watching his back. Not for the knife. For the razor.

The fact that he tended to elaborate on or improvise on the Bureau's standard operating procedures also hadn't made him many friends in high places.

That the Section had been reinstated was a stroke of good fortune, but he never gloated.

He did his job.

Looking.

Always looking.

Following the crooked path.

He wandered around to the back of the statue, tracing his fingers along the marble base.

What he wanted to do now was make sure that this Louisiana thing was weird stuff, nothing more.

He had to be sure that he wasn't so desperate that he saw only what he wanted to see, not what was really there.

Not so easy to do these days, when he had been so close.

So damn close.

He stepped back as he slipped into his jacket and looked up at the president, dark bronze and gleaming, towering above him.

"So what do you think?" he said quietly. "You bought the stupid place, is there anything out there?"

A hand gripped his shoulder.

When he tried to turn, the grip tightened, ordering him to stay where he was.

His throat dried instantly, but he did as he was bidden. He wasn't afraid, just wary.

He lowered his head slowly to keep his neck from cramping.

The hand didn't move, nor did it relax its grip.

"Well?" he asked mildly.

Mint; he smelled an aftershave or cologne with a faint touch of mint, and the warmth of the sun on someone's clothes, as if he'd walked a long way to reach him. The hand was strong, but he couldn't see it without turning his head.

"Mr. Mulder." A smooth voice, not very deep.

He nodded. He was patient. Not often, however; both his temper and his temperament never had liked short leashes. He tried to adjust his shoulder, but the fingers wouldn't let him.

"Louisiana," the voice said, fading slightly, telling him the man had turned his head. "It's not what you hope, but you shouldn't ignore it."

"Mind if I ask who you are?" Still mild, still calm.

"Yes."

"Mind if I ask if—"

"Yes."

The grip tightened, pinching a nerve that made Mulder's eyes close briefly. He nodded, once. He understood—*keep your mouth shut, ask no questions, pay attention.*

Voices approached outside—children, for a change sounding respectful, not rowdy.

A car's horn blared.

"The fact, Mr. Mulder, that your Section has been reactivated does not mean there still aren't those who would like to make sure you stay out of their way. Permanently." A shift of cloth, and the voice was closer, a harsh whisper in his left ear. "You're still not protected, Mr Mulder, but you're not in chains, either. Remember that. You'll have to."

The grip tightened again, abruptly, just as the voices entered the memorial and turned to echoes. His eyes instantly filled with tears, and his knees buckled as he cried out softly. A lunge with his arm couldn't prevent his forehead from slamming against the pedestal as he went down. By the time his vision cleared, no more than a few seconds, he was kneeling, head down, and when he looked to his right, grimacing, the only person he saw was a little girl with an ice cream cone, braids, and a vivid blue jumper.

"Are you okay, Mister?" she asked, licking at the cone.

He touched his shoulder gingerly, swallowed a curse, and managed a nod while taking several deep breaths.

A woman appeared behind the girl, gently easing her away. "Sir, do you need help?"

He looked up at her and smiled. "Just felt a little dizzy, that's all." Bracing one hand against the pedestal got him to his feet. The woman and the girl, and about a dozen others, backed away warily as he moved. "Thanks," he said to the woman.

She nodded politely.

He stepped outside.

The breeze attacked his forelock, and he swiped at it absently as he slipped into his jacket. His shoulder stung, but he barely noticed it. What he did notice was the breath of ice across the back of his neck.

Whoever the man was, there had been no threats, but there had been no promises either.

And for the first time in a long time, he felt that tiny rush of excitement that told him the hunt was on again.

Not the hunt for the bad guys.

The hunt for the truth.

THREE

Corporal Frank Ulman was tired of lying in bed. His back was sore, his ass was sore, his legs were sore. The only thing that wasn't sore was his head, and he figured that would fall off if he had to count the holes in the ceiling one more time.

It was, no question about it, a lousy way to spend a Saturday night.

What made it worse was the fact that he was here because he had been stupid. Really stupid. All he had wanted last night was a quiet drink, pick up someone for the evening because his regular girl had to work, and wake up the next day without a hangover. No big deal. So he had wrangled a pass from the sarge, no sweat, put on his civies, and hitched a ride into Marville with a couple of half-bald Warrant Officers who spent the whole time bitching about the way the DoD couldn't make up its mind whether to close Dix down or not.

They had dropped him off at Barney's Tavern.

He went in and had his drink, passed a few words with the muscle-bound bartender, watched a couple of innings of Phillies baseball on the TV, and listened while the curiously noisy crowd gabbed about old Grady getting his throat slashed the weekend before.

It was a shame. He had kind of liked the old fart, had bought him a drink now and then, and enjoyed listening to his stories. Grady had called him "Sal," because, he said, Frankie looked like some old actor or something named Sal Mineo. After the first couple of times, Frankie hadn't bothered to correct him. If the old guy thought he looked like a movie star, it was no skin off his nose.

Now that Grady was dead, so was Sal.

Too bad.

Another drink, another inning, and he made his first mistake: He tried to pick up a woman sitting by herself at a table near the back. Not bad looking in the tavern's twilight, but he wasn't about to be fussy. Angie wasn't here, and he was. Just like always. It was a mistake because the bitch didn't want to be picked up, said so loudly when he persisted, and finally suggested that he perform a certain number of mind-boggling, and definitely unnatural, sexual acts upon himself on his way home to his momma.

His second mistake was dropping a twenty on the table in front of her and telling her to either put up or shut up, and don't forget the change.

His third mistake was not listening to that muscle-bound bartender, who told him to get his sorry ass out of his bar before the roof fell in.

Corporal Ulman, with too many boilermakers and a hell of an attitude under his belt, called the bartender a fag.

The next thing he knew he was in Walson, the Air Force hospital on post, getting stitched under the chin, getting a cast on his left arm, and getting a facefull of the sarge, who had been waiting for him when the cops brought him in.

Bed rest was the order, take these pills, stay out of trouble, don't come back.

All day he stared at the barracks ceiling, his left arm throbbing in a sling, his face a road map of yellow and purple bruises.

Nobody felt sorry for him.

The sarge had told him that when he got up the next day, he was going to be busted. Again.

So he figured he didn't have a whole hell of a lot to lose when he swung his legs over the side of the bed and waited for the dizziness to pass. He had to get out. Walk around a little. Get some fresh air. Maybe find a card game and tell a few stories of his own. Anything but count those damn holes again.

Clumsily he dressed in boots and fatigues, made it as far as the door before he felt the first ache, deep in his jawbone. It almost sent him back, but now it was a matter of pride. A busted arm, a few bruises, what kind of a soldier would he be if he let something like that keep him on his back?

He checked the second floor corridor and saw no one, heard nothing. Why should he? Everyone else was having a good time, bumping around Marville, Browns Mills, drinking themselves blind, getting laid, catching a flick.

The thought made him angry.

One goddamn lucky punch, one lousy mistake, and here he was, practically a cripple. And he wouldn't put it past one of the guys to call Angie and tell her everything.

Son of a bitch.

What he needed, he decided then, wasn't a card game, it was a drink. Something to calm him down, something to ease the pain.

He knew just where to get it.

Five minutes later, after slipping a cheap and slim flashlight into his hip pocket and dry-swallowing one of the pain pills the doc had given him, he was in and out of Howie Jacker's room, two pints of Southern Comfort tucked into his shirt. The jerk never learned to lock his locker, his loss, Frankie's gain.

Five minutes after that he was outside. Behind the brick barracks the woods began, and he slipped into them quickly, making his way along a well-worn path toward a clearing half a mile in. He'd been invited there last summer, a place reserved for those who wanted to drink, or whatever, alone, without the hassle of officially leaving the post.

Actually, the clearing was beyond the post's boundary, which meant that its users were technically AWOL.

Not that anybody cared.

One part of these damn woods was the same as another.

He took the first sip almost before the barracks lights were blocked by the trees, gasping at the hundred-proof sweetness, smacking his lips as the throbbing began to fade. This was a great idea, and beat counting holes all to hell and gone. He took another drink, tucked the pint into the sling, and pulled out the flash. The beam was narrow, but he only needed it to warn him of pine boughs and oak branches. The trail itself had been used so often, it was practically a ditch.

He moved quickly, glancing up now and then in hopes of seeing the stars or the moon. It wasn't that he was afraid of the woods. Not really. For a city boy, he had learned to take them or leave them.

What he didn't like was the voice the trees had.

When the breeze blew, there were whispers, like old men talking about him behind their hands; when the air was still, the leaves still moved, nudged by night things who stayed just out of reach of the narrow white beam.

He drank again.

The woods talked to him.

He stopped once and checked behind him, slashing the beam up the trail, seeing nothing but grey trunks and colorless underbrush.

He drank, walked, and cursed when he realized the first pint was already empty. He tossed the bottle aside angrily, took out the second one, and slipped it into the sling. Later; that one was for later.

The breeze kicked into a gust of strong wind, damp and cool.

The branches danced and whispered.

Okay, he thought, so maybe not such a hot idea after all. Maybe he should just go back, lay down, drink himself into a stupor and let the sarge do his worst in the morning.

His head ached, his arm ached, his jaw ached.

"Jesus," he muttered.

Another gust shoved him off the trail, the beam blurring across the ground, sparkling as it passed through pockets of mist.

Something moved, out there in the dark.

Something large.

Frankie swayed, wishing he hadn't drunk so much, wishing he hadn't taken those pills first.

His stomach felt on fire, and sweat had broken out across his brow and down his spine.

It wasn't warm at all.

The wind had turned cold.

He heard it again, something moving toward him, not bothering to mask its approach.

His first thought was *Jersey Devil*, and he giggled. Right. A real live monster in the middle of New Jersey. Right. Tell me another.

His stomach lurched.

He swallowed hard and hurried on, swerving around a bush whose thorns clawed at his legs. His broken arm burned now, too, and he cradled it with his free hand, sending the beam sideways, poking at the black without pushing it away.

When he collided with a sapling that threw him to the ground, he cried out, cursed, kicked himself awkwardly to his feet and demanded to know who the hell was out there, he was a sick man, he was lost, goddamnit, and he didn't need this shit.

The wind tugged at his hair, plucked at his shirt.

A drop of rain splattered on the tip of nose.

"Oh great," he muttered. "That's just fucking great."

Something in the trees overhead.

Something in the dark just behind.

He wiped his face with a forearm, used the flashlight like a lance as he found a clear path and broke into a slow trot. It wasn't the right trail, but it had to lead somewhere, and right now somewhere other than here was exactly where he wanted to be.

Stupid; he was stupid.

The sarge was going to kill him, Angie was going to kill him, and Howie would definitely kill him when he found his stash gone.

Something behind.

Something above.

Light rain slipped between the leaves, between the branches.

God, he thought, get me outta here.

He swerved easily around a gnarled oak, dodged the grasp of a cage of white birch. He couldn't hear anything but his own breathing now, and the wind, and the patter of the rain, but he couldn't stop running. Every step exploded in his arm, but he couldn't stop running, following the sweep and dart of the beam until he rounded a thicket and the ground was gone.

He yelled as he tumbled into a ditch, screamed when he landed on his arm, and blacked out until the pain brought him back.

Rain on his face, like the touch of spider legs.

He rolled onto his knees and hand, and threw up until his throat burned. Then he rocked back on his heels, amazed that the flashlight was still in his grip. He used it to check the ditch, saw it was barely three feet deep.

And there was a road.

"All right!"

Dizzy, swallowing rapidly, he staggered to his feet and looked back at the woods.

No way. No way. He would hike until someone found him, or he found a way back to the post. If it was an MP patrol, who cared? Anything was better than this. Even the sarge.

He slipped-crawled up the other side and onto the tarmac, took a deep breath, and began walking.

The ditch ended a few yards later, the trees closing in, not even leaving a shoulder.

It didn't take long before the pain finally reasserted itself and he had to stop, lean against a dead pine whose branches had been stripped off all the way to the top. There were several of them here, and he figured it was lightning, a quick fire; there was a lot of patches like this here in the Barrens.

"Okay," he said. "Okay, move your butt."

Maybe a drink.

One drink.

The rain was cold and the wind was cold and he was too cold for a spring night like this. He reached into the sling, and laughed when he pulled out the second pint, intact.

He unscrewed the cap and lifted the bottle in a toast to the sky.

He drank and licked his lips.

He lowered his head and saw the outline of a covered Jeep not fifty yards ahead, parked on the left.

He grinned, waved the flashlight, and started up the road, every few feet bracing himself against one of the trees. It wasn't the MPs, thank God. Probably somebody out to get a little with a townie. He laughed. A Jeep, while it was possible, was hardly the best way in the world.

He drank and waved the flashlight again.

The passenger door swung open, and he saw a woman's face.

"Hey!" he called. Hiccuped. "Give a guy a lift?"

The woman's face disappeared.

He drank and grinned, stumbled, and reached out to catch himself on a trunk.

The wood was soft.

Too soft.

He yelped and jumped back, the bottle dropping from his hand.

He aimed the flashlight unsteadily, and saw the arm reach out of the bark.

He saw the blade.

He heard himself scream.

But he could only scream once.

FOUR

Mulder freely admitted to anyone who asked that his office, such as it was, seldom complied, strictly or otherwise, with regulations. While he knew where everything was, usually, it wasn't always where Bureau Section Heads decreed it ought to be. Controlled tornado was how one of his friends had put it; a hell of a mess was how he described it. Usually with a shrug. Always without apology. Nevertheless, despite the fact that it was in the basement of the J. Edgar Hoover Building, it served its purpose; and the fact that he still had it after all the waves he had made over previous X-File cases was, to more than a few, a minor miracle.

He sat there now, chair tilted back as he

wadded up blank sheets of paper and tossed them toward a metal wastebasket set in front of a pair of brown metal file cabinets. "Toward" was the right word. "Into" would have been nicer, but that rarely happened.

Like visiting with Jefferson, it helped him think.

Today, it also helped him kill time while waiting to be summoned to his appointment with his new immediate superior, Arlen Douglas. The word on the floor was, the man, even though he was only in the slot temporarily, wasn't pleased with the success rate of his agents, and he was hunting for scalps.

Which was why the floor in front of his filing cabinets looked like a snowfield when Carl Barelli walked in, visitor's pass clipped to his sports jacket's breast pocket.

Mulder tossed, missed, swiveled his chair around and said, "Michael Jordan is safe for another season."

"Jordan retired last year."

Mulder rolled his eyes. "That's the trouble with you, Carl. You pay too much attention to details. It's the big picture you have to consider."

To his surprise, his old friend didn't respond. Instead, he wandered around the room, fingers drifting but touching nothing, glancing at without really seeing the charts and Most Wanted sheets, the notes and NASA posters taped and tacked to the wall.

He was a swarthy man with thick black hair and a classic Italian profile dented and scarred just enough to prevent him from being pretty. He was also a former semi-pro footballer who had all the heart and few of the major skills to make it in the NFL or Canada. Luckily, he had recognized the shortcomings before it was too late; now he wrote about the sport for the revitalized *New Jersey Chronicle*, and once every six weeks or so came down to Washington to check out the Redskins, or to see what Congress was up to with a recent flurry of sports safety legislation. While he was here, he always dropped in, looking for a free meal, or a long night of pub-crawling.

Mulder never asked how his friend always managed to get a pass without calling ahead; he had a feeling he didn't need to know the answer.

"So," Barelli said, finally lighting on a chair, kicking aside the paper balls as he stretched out his legs. He glanced through the doorway to the quiet flow of agents outside, then back at the walls.

"So," Mulder echoed.

"So where's Scully?"

"She took some time off. She went West someplace, to see friends, I think. She's too cheap to send me a postcard." A shrug with his eyebrows. "Today's Wednesday, the fifth, right? She'll be back on Monday."

"Too bad. I could've saved her."

Mulder smiled, but it wasn't wide, merely

polite. Carl had been trying to get Scully out of the Bureau and into his love life, not necessarily in that order, ever since he had met her just over a year ago. Scully, although she claimed to be flattered by the attention, didn't think this was the guy who would, as she put it, light up her life.

Neither did Mulder.

While he liked Carl a lot, and they had good times together, the man was incorrigible and unrepentant when it came to chasing women. As far as Mulder was concerned, Scully was permanently out of bounds.

Barelli folded his hands over his stomach, pursed his lips, licked them, blew out a silent whistle.

"What?" Mulder was puzzled. No handshake, no raucous invitation to debauchery, no futile attempt to show him exactly how to shoot a basket. The established routine had been abandoned, and he didn't care for the way the man refused to meet his gaze.

The reporter shook himself elaborately, forced a smile, crossed his legs. "Sorry, pal. To be honest, I've had a pretty shitty week, all in all, and it sure ain't getting any better sitting in this place. When the hell are you going to get a room with a view?"

"I like it here. It's quiet."

"It's like a tomb is what it is."

Mulder didn't take the bait. "What's the problem, Carl?"

The man hesitated before clearing his throat. "You remember Frank Ulman?"

Mulder wadded up another sheet. "No, I don't think so. Should I?"

"He was at my sister's a couple of Christmases ago. Skinny kid? Regular Army? He kept hitting on my cousin Angie, she kept shooting him down, and you decided to show him how to do it right."

Suddenly, as he threw the paper ball, he remembered the night, and the memory brought a smile. The kid, and he wasn't much more than that, had paraded around the Barellis' suburban North Jersey house in his dress uniform, desperately trying to find a woman who would be impressed by his bearing and ribbons. He was so eager, he was laughable, and Mulder had finally taken pity on him. Unfortunately, the heart-to-heart they had had in the rec room didn't take. Barelli's cousin's brother had had to be physically restrained from punching the guy into the new year.

"Yeah," he said, nodding. "Yeah."

The ball went in.

"Well, a couple, three months ago, he and Angie got together. Kind of serious, actually. I heard they were talking marriage and stuff."

Mulder's eyes widened. "Your cousin and that guy? Really? Why didn't her brother kill him?"

Barelli winced and looked away.

Oh shit, Mulder thought; open mouth, insert foot.

He abandoned his slouch for a posture more attentive. "Tell me."

"He was killed last weekend."

"Damn. Hey, I'm sorry, Carl. I didn't mean—"

Barelli waved him silent. "It's okay, don't sweat it, you couldn't have known." His smile was bitter. "Not exactly national news, you know?" Then he inhaled slowly. "The thing is, Mulder, he was stationed at Fort Dix, some kind of pissant clerical job, even though he thought he should have been something else. You know, glamorous? Green Berets, something like that. Anyway, he got himself into a fight at a bar in a nearby town, they call it Marville—"

"Over a woman, I'll bet."

"Yeah. Something like that. Anyway, he ended up at the base hospital Friday night, busted up some, and was supposed to stay in bed until Sunday. Frankie didn't want to stay in bed, apparently. He was found on a road just south of the post, on Sunday morning."

"How?"

Barelli swiped at something invisible on his shirtfront. "Somebody cut his throat."

Mulder closed his eyes briefly, both in sympathy and at the image. "Have they caught the one who did it?"

"No."

"Witnesses?"

The man snorted. "Oh yeah, right. In the middle of the night out in the middle of nowhere? Jesus, Mulder, gimme a break." Then he shrugged. "Yeah. Actually, there was one. A woman." He leaned forward, bracing his arms on his legs. "But Jesus, Mulder, she was hysterical and drunk and maybe doped up. You know what she said? She said the damn tree grew an arm and killed him."

Arlen Douglas could have been anywhere from his early forties to early sixties. His perpetually tanned face was finely lined, his hair an aristocratic mix of brown and silver, and his figure one of someone who was in close to perfect shape. He sat behind his desk and took a single swipe at his tie before closing the manila folder that lay before him on the leather-trim blotter.

It hadn't taken him long to make the office his—framed photographs of his family on the desk, framed photographs of him and three presidents, a handful of movie stars, and a dozen senators on the walls. An American flag in a brass stand to the right. Behind him, a large window whose view of the city was cut off by pale beige blinds.

When his intercom buzzed, he touched a button, said, "Send him in, Miss Cort," and checked his tie again.

Special Agent Webber opened the door hesitantly, smiled, and stepped across the threshold.

Another hesitation before he closed the door and marched to the desk.

Douglas prayed that the kid wouldn't salute him.

"You sent for me, sir?"

"Indeed I did, Hank." He tapped the folder. "A fine job your team did on that Helevito case. A very nice job indeed."

Webber beamed. "Thank you, sir. But it wasn't really my team, it was Agent Mulder's."

Douglas smiled without showing any teeth. "Of course. But it seems you came up with a vital piece of the puzzle, and exhibited some very fine investigative techniques."

He waited while the young man did his best to contain his pleasure. This, he thought, was going to be a piece of cake.

"Tell me something, Hank, how did you like working with Fox Mulder?"

"Oh, boy," Webber said enthusiastically. "It was great. I mean, they teach you all that stuff at Quantico, but it doesn't really have anything to do with . . ." He stopped himself and frowned briefly. "What I mean, sir, isn't that Quantico doesn't do its job. Not at all. I mean—"

"I know what you mean," Douglas said, still smiling, hands now flat on the folder. "It doesn't come alive, does it, until you actually see it all in action."

"Yes, sir. Exactly."

Well, of course, it doesn't, you idiot, he

thought. Someone was going to owe him big time for this. Real big time.

"And you found working with Mulder instructive?"

"Absolutely."

"By the book, everything in its place, nothing for anyone to be ashamed of?"

He knew the young man would falter, and he did, torn between his liking for Mulder and his loyalty to the Bureau. Douglas was well aware that Mulder used the book when he had to, and his own, rather unique experience when necessary. The problem was, that experience. Half the time, it seemed like nothing but hunches; the other half consisted of such wild speculation that Douglas was amazed the man had any arrest record at all.

He waved a dismissive hand. "Never mind, Hank. It's not really important." He slid his hands off the folder. "As I said, this is fine work. Thanks to you, we should have no trouble in court putting Helevito away for most of the rest of his life." The smile faded to an expression that was both an invitation to the inner circle and a warning against betrayed confidences. "But before you decide to make Mulder your hero, there's something you should know."

Webber frowned his puzzlement.

"And something I'd like you to do for me." The smile returned, this time with teeth. "A personal favor. One, I think, which will not hinder your advancement in the Bureau one iota."

Mulder wasn't sure what he was supposed to say next. He had already explained to Barelli as carefully as he could that he couldn't take on the case without authorization, or without a request from the local law enforcement agency, but the reporter refused to accept it. He kept insisting this was Mulder's kind of thing, right up his alley.

Weird stuff, Mulder thought sourly; famous throughout the whole damn world for weird stuff.

"It doesn't matter," he said, making sure Carl heard and saw the regret. "You said yourself the woman had been drinking. And was hysterical. As anyone very well might be who had witnessed something sudden and gruesome like that. Which is why, believe it or not, eyewitnesses aren't always the best way to pursue a case. Get three people at the scene of a violent crime like this, and I'll guarantee three different versions of what happened."

"Look, Fox, I know—"

Mulder held up a palm. "What I'm saying is, Carl, that this woman was obviously severely shaken up. Like I said, anyone would be, and—"

"Speak for yourself," a dry voice said from the doorway.

Barelli instantly leapt to his feet, a great, wolfish smile cracking his solemnity. "Dana! Darlin'!"

Mulder merely looked to the door. "You're back early."

Dana Scully made a face, tossed her purse at him and shrugged out of her light topcoat. "I got back last night. I got tired of looking at interstates. After a few days they're all the same—boring. And very exhausting."

She didn't look exhausted to him. Her light auburn hair was in place, her slightly rounded face clear of any hint of weariness, and her clothes—a ruffled blouse and wine-colored jacket with matching skirt—were impeccable.

As practically always.

"You look perfect," Barelli said, crossed the room and engulfed her in a hug.

"Hi, Carl." She accepted the hug for only a few seconds, then slipped out of it so deftly Mulder wanted to applaud.

He nodded toward his friend instead. "Carl has a problem, but I'm afraid we can't help him."

"Bullshit." Barelli laughed heartily. "You just need some convincing, that's all. And this is just the little lady who can do it."

Scully avoided another hug by catching the purse Mulder tossed back to her and, at the same time, preempting the other chair.

"So how was the trip?"

She took her time answering. "Nice. Very relaxing."

"You should have stayed the whole time."

"What, are you kidding?" Barelli folded his

arms and leaned against the jamb. "You don't know that little lady very well, Mulder. Can't keep her mind off business for more than two hours at a time." His smile was seductive, he knew it, and he used it. "Which makes me glad to see you, Dana. Maybe you can talk this guy into giving a friend a hand."

Scully quickly glared at Mulder, who had already raised his hands to offer mock applause. Instead the right hand shot to scratch at the back of his head, while the left answered the perfectly timed ringing phone beside him.

He listened.

He watched Dana watching him.

He hung up and said, "Carl, I'm sorry, but I have to see the boss" as he rose and reached for his suit jacket. "Let Dana know where you're staying and I'll call you later."

"Mulder?" Dana frowned.

"No, don't worry, I'm not in trouble." He paused at the door. "I don't think I'm in trouble." He stepped over the threshold and looked over his shoulder. "How can I be in trouble? We just closed a big case."

FIVE

Diamond Street was barely wide enough for two lanes of traffic on its easy downward slope toward the Potomac River. Richly crowned hickory and maple lined the worn curbs, hiding for most of its length old and small, brick and clapboard homes with front lawns scarcely large enough for the name. At the top of the slope were a handful of businesses, spillovers from South Washington Street. On the west side was Ripley's, flanked on the left by a corner grocery, and on the right by a narrow three-story Victorian converted to a dress shop on the ground floor, law offices above. The bar's simple brick facade was deliberately no advertisement; all there was was a dark green padded door over which hung a

THE X-FILES

scripted sign in red. No window large or small. It was a neighborhood bar, no outsiders or the outside need apply.

Mulder stepped in and immediately stripped off his coat, sighing a little, pushing a weary hand through his hair. To his left were a half-dozen small tables, already taken; to his right, a wall covered above dark wood wainscoting with film and old radio show posters framed in polished wood. As soon as his vision adjusted to the dim lighting, all except for the bar itself from short candles in amber chimneys on the tables and sconces on the walls, he moved slowly toward the back, down a narrow aisle created where the mahogany bar began. That was filled too, but the noise level was low.

Conversation, quiet laughter, a few nods and smiles in his direction.

When the bar ended, the room opened up into a large square, with more tables, and high-backed booths settled against the walls. There was no TV, no jukebox; the background music piped through hidden speakers was barely loud enough to register. Sometimes it was country, sometimes jazz, sometimes themes from films and Broadway shows. It all depended on the mood Stuff Felstead was in when he opened for lunch.

It didn't take Mulder long to recognize the soundtrack from *Alien*. Stuff had apparently seen him coming.

46

With a grin he swung left and dropped into the booth nearest the end of the bar, shifted, and sat with his back against the wall, one leg stretched out on the padded seat, his topcoat dumped on the other seat. Within seconds, a tall woman stood in front of him, in loose black slacks, puff-sleeved white blouse. Black Irish from head to toe—hair, eyes, fair skin, a faint suggestion of freckles across her upturned nose.

"Are you dead or drinking?"

He rolled his eyes and groaned. "Both, I think."

"Beer?"

He nodded.

She winked and drifted away.

He covered his eyes with his left hand, elbow propped on the table, and wondered if maybe he had slipped into some alternate time zone, some parallel universe.

All the signs were there: Arlen Douglas hadn't kept him waiting, but had personally ushered him into his office. Congratulations on the Helevito case were suspiciously effusive, as was praise for taking such good care of Hank Webber. Mulder hadn't had a chance to say a word save a murmur of thanks before the Section Head asked him what he thought about the disappearing clown.

"A trick, obviously."

"What makes you think so?"

"He's not the Invisible Man, sir. Nobody can snap his fingers and vanish."

"Intriguing, though, don't you think?"

He heard the warning bells immediately and did his best to avoid what he feared was coming, pointing out suspect witnesses, the very backdrop of the circus, incomplete preliminary reports from the local sheriff . . .

It didn't work.

He had one day to finish the Helevito paperwork, and then he was off to Louisiana over the weekend.

"Just up your alley, wouldn't you say, Agent Mulder?"

Mulder had wanted to say, "Up your alley, too. Sir." But a sudden attack of restraint kept him silent as he was handed a blue-tabbed case folder and ushered back out before he had a chance to continue his objections.

It wasn't until he'd returned to his empty office and flipped through the pages that he realized Scully wouldn't be going with him. Hank Webber would.

This wasn't right. Not that he didn't mind shepherding the younger man through the minefields of Bureau investigations; that was the least of his problems, and Webber was a personable, if somewhat overenthusiastic man.

What wasn't right was the smell of it. Right up his alley, the man had said. Weird stuff. But this wasn't weird at all; it was just nuts, and he wondered exactly who had asked for the FBI to join in what looked to be an obvious local matter.

Plus, let's not forget the man at the Memorial. Invisible as well, and all too real.

Not protected, but not chained.

Alice was right—curiouser and curiouser.

Parallel universe; it had to be.

"If it's that bad, maybe I'll bring hemlock for a chaser."

He opened his eyes and kept his expression bland as the waitress set a bottle of beer on the table, along with a plate filled with french fries. He pointed. "I didn't order those, Trudy."

"You haven't eaten."

Their aroma made his stomach growl, and she laughed silently when he reached for one and popped it into his mouth, hissing as it burned his tongue. Reluctantly, stiffly, he swung his leg back under the table and saw that a thick, all-the-trimmings hamburger had been buried beneath the fries. He looked at her sideways, and she winked again before heading across the room at a customer's call.

He didn't hide his interest. She was an attractive woman, a law student now at Georgetown, and they had dated a couple of times, nothing fancy, nothing hot. He enjoyed her and her company, although he couldn't always take her mothering. Tonight, however, it was right on target, and he ate as if he hadn't done so in a week, ordering a second burger before he'd finished the first. Taking his time. No hurry at all.

Because it was the middle of the week, the room didn't fill. The booths were taken first, and a handful of tables changed occupants once or twice as he watched them. Mostly younger people back here; the old-timers stuck to the stools where they were closer to what mattered.

A couple of times women seated close by would glance at him, glance away, glance back, but he didn't acknowledge them and so lost their interest. Two men in golf caps and cardigans argued quietly at a table with someone in a booth he couldn't see. A married couple dressed more for the theater than Ripley's fussed unhappily with kaiser roll sandwiches. A quartet of college kids tried to pick Trudy and the other two waitresses up.

A normal night.

In a parallel universe.

Oh, brother, he thought; maybe it's time I took a vacation.

A room whose walls weren't all the same color, mostly shadow now, mostly dark.

On the right-hand wall a dark-framed print, Gainesborough's *The Blue Boy*, fronted with nonreflective glass.

Against the left-hand wall, a bunk with a thin mattress, blanket and sheet drawn taut and folded in the military style. A footlocker at the head, closed, chipped and scarred.

GOBLINS

A metal desk set perpendicular to the rear wall. On it two piles of paperback books, a stackable stereo system, a handful of compact discs. A yellow legal pad, with a ballpoint pen just off-center. A green-shaded lamp, softly lit. A swivel chair whose seat and back were comfortably padded.

In the far corner a club chair, with a standing brass lamp behind it, an end table beside it with a seashell ashtray.

The floor was concrete, uncarpeted save for a remnant throw in front of the chair.

A man in a long lab coat wandered around the room, poking at the books, the CDs, scowling at the legal pad whose top sheet was blank, picking up the pen, stabbing the page lightly before dropping it again. Although he was only in his mid-forties, he had more scalp than hair, his face sharp angles without seeming harsh. When he straightened, he was tall, broad at the shoulders and chest, and broad at his stomach. He glanced around, his nose wrinkling at the faint stench of cigarette smoke and mildew, sweat and blood, and finally, with a satisfied nod, strode to a padded door in the wall. He opened it without hesitation and stepped up into a corridor whose ceiling lighting was contrast enough to force a squint as he checked through the round judas window before turning right and stepping up into the next room, itself dimly lighted.

"Ready?" A woman in white sat at a wall-long

shelf on which was a series of monitors and keyboards, space for notebooks and pads, and two styrofoam cups of steaming coffee.

The shelf was set just beneath a window that looked through the ghost of the Blue Boy, down into the other room.

"Leonard, I asked if you were ready." Long blond hair pulled back and held back by a rubber band, feathered bangs on a high forehead.

Leonard Tymons, when he had first met her, thought Rosemary Elkhart quite attractive in a hard sort of way. After four years he hadn't changed his mind, but he had changed his plans for seduction and a brief affair. She indeed did have fair hair and fair skin, pale lips and pale blue eyes, but when he was alone he called her a black widow.

"Leonard, damnit."

He dropped into a wheeled chair beside her. "You saw."

She nodded toward a microphone attached to one of the computers. "For the record, okay? Let's remember the record."

He nodded. "For the record, everything is fine. Nothing has changed since last time. Jesus, can't we get anyone to clean that place right? It smells like a . . . a . . ." He shook his head in disgust. "Just get someone to scrub it down before next time."

"I will."

There was silence then as they worked at

their keyboards, setting programs in motion, for the moment paying little attention to the diagrams and numbers that flashed across the screens.

Then Tymons reached out and flicked off the mike.

Rosemary looked at him oddly.

"We blew it, didn't we," he said matter-of-factly. A tilt of his head toward the glass. "We're not going to bring it off, are we?"

Her face hardened as if she were about to lose her temper, and for several seconds she refused to answer.

"Rosemary."

She sagged, and whispered, "Damn."

The soft hum of fans, the creak of his chair's wheels as he pushed away from the shelf desk and rubbed his face with both hands.

"Maybe," she said, "there's a way."

"Maybe," he answered, "there's a Santa Claus."

Her face hardened again, and she gestured him back to his position. "Santa Claus or not," she told him, "we will find a way." She glanced at him sideways. "If not, we'll just get another."

The music had changed to the muted soundtrack from *Damn Yankees* when Trudy Gaines slipped into the seat opposite Mulder, lit a cigarette, and brushed a strand of damp hair from her brow as she blew smoke at the ceiling. "One day, he's going to find everyone in here puddled on his precious floor."

Mulder raised an eyebrow. "You're warm?" He hadn't noticed.

She nodded, and even in the gloom he could see the lines, the shadows, that made her more her age. "I think I'm getting the flu or something."

He finished the last burger, picked up his second beer. "So take a day off."

"You pay my rent?"

"You give me that autographed *Thing From Another World* poster?"

"In your dreams, G-man. In your dreams."

The Golf Caps' argument grew louder.

"Jesus," she muttered.

"What's up?" The person in the booth was still in shadow; all he could see was one arm, in a tweed, elbow-patched sleeve.

"The Redskins," she said in disgust.

He couldn't help a laugh. "What? May's just started, for God's sake."

She looked at him with one eye open. "It's always autumn when you're a Redskins fan, Mulder, don't you know that?"

One of the Golf Caps stood, his chair scraping back. Before anyone could move, a man in shirtsleeves, a white apron tied around his waist, appeared by the table. He was, Mulder thought, the perfect walking cadaver. Only the badly arthritic hands spoiled the image. Evidently the

Golf Cap didn't think Stuff Felstead could do anything but glower. He was wrong. Ripley's owner said something so low only the other man could hear. It was enough. He sputtered, gestured placatingly, and by his expression suggested to his companion that they leave.

It was over in less than ten seconds.

"Magic," Trudy said, catching him staring.

"Probably. After all this time, I still don't see how he does it."

"Keep it that way," she advised him. "Believe me, you don't want to know." She set her palms flat on the table. "Well, break's over. Gotta finish up."

"Nice visiting with you, too," he said, sweeping up the last of the ketchup with the last french fry. "So what's the problem?"

She froze halfway out of the booth, avoiding his gaze, staring at the seatback behind him.

He waited.

Finally, she slumped back and shook her head. "It's silly."

"Probably."

"I feel like a jerk."

He reached out his hand and waggled it until she handed him his coat. "You're off in ten minutes, you've had another fight with your boyfriend, you have a tort quiz tomorrow, and you want a walk home in case he tries to hassle you."

She didn't blink. "You know, Mulder, sometimes you're damn weird."

He shrugged. "So they tell me."

"Fifteen minutes?"

"Sure. No problem."

A quick smile was her thanks as she returned to work, and fifteen minutes later she was back, heavy sweater over her arm. He paid at the register at the end of the bar and followed her to the street. His own apartment was a couple of blocks past King Street, closer to the Potomac; she lived the same distance in the opposite direction. He didn't mind. It was a nice night, a comfortable breeze, and Trudy spent most of the time complaining about her landlady in a way that, at one point, had him laughing so hard he tripped over a raised section of sidewalk.

He didn't fall. A quick, exaggerated turn kept his balance.

But not so quick that he didn't see the man in the tweed jacket strolling behind them a block away.

It didn't register at first because they had already reached her place, a renovated colonial divided into a half-dozen apartments, hidden beneath a clutch of oaks. She kissed his cheek quickly for thanks and hurried up the walk, fussing in her purse for the keys.

He didn't leave until the front door was open and she was inside.

Then he turned around and headed back the way they had come, hands in his pockets, whistling softly. His footsteps were loud. Traffic didn't exist. A dog raced silently across a sloped lawn to check him out, tail wagging, fangs bared. Mulder gave the animal a smile and walked on.

Checking the shadows for a shadow that didn't belong.

By the time he had crossed King Street again, he had begun to scold himself. After all, people had to live someplace, some of them actually lived in the same area he did, and the Tweed Man was probably one of them.

His own building was on a quiet residential street. Well-kept dark brick with a slight arch over the recessed entrance. Hedges that made the tiny lawn seem even smaller. As he slipped his keys out of his pocket, he began making a list of things he'd have to do in the morning, not the least of which would be to try to change Douglas's mind.

A disappearing murderous clown was not his idea of a good reason to see Louisiana.

By the time he reached the door he was already in bed; all he had to do was get his body settled in the same place.

He turned the lock and absently glanced over his shoulder.

The Tweed Man strolled by on the other side of the street, cigarette in one hand tracing orange in the dark, face hidden by a felt hat pulled low.

Weariness slowed Mulder's reaction. In the few seconds it took to convince himself he wasn't imagining it, the man was gone, lost in the shifting shadows between widely spaced streetlamps.

SIX

Dana Scully stood amid the clutter of Mulder's office and flapped her arms hopelessly. There were times when she admired the way he could find needles in haystacks and times like this, when she wanted nothing more than to put a match to it and force him to start from scratch. Which, she knew, wouldn't change a thing. Two days later it would look just the same.

Hefting her briefcase in one hand, she turned with a resigned sigh to the woman standing in the doorway and said, "Sorry, Bette, but I don't think it's here."

"Sure it is," the secretary said brightly. She crossed the room to a waist-high shelf built out of the wall, shoved a pile of papers aside and held up a blue-tagged folder. "I can smell 'em a mile away."

A cheery smile, and she was gone, leaving Scully openmouthed and slightly annoyed. She didn't mind cases being targeted to other teams; that was part of the game, and part of the procedure. And that particular case was, by FBI standards, so perfectly ordinary she was surprised Mulder hadn't pushed it on himself. What she did mind was the new Section Head's near-imperious refusal to give his reasons. If he wasn't happy with the way things were going, he simply changed teams. Fresh minds and fresh bodies was his only explanation.

"Hey."

Mulder came through the door, dropped his coat onto the back of his chair. "Listen, I've been thinking about that Louisiana thing."

Dana shook her head. "Mulder—"

He dropped into his chair, swiveled it around to face her, and tented his fingers beneath his chin. "Not that I think it's really going to be as bizarre as the mighty Douglas thinks it is, but I've been looking through the folder, see . . ." He reached over to the shelf without looking. "I think what they've got there is a—"

"Mulder—"

He frowned, kicked the chair around, and began slapping papers aside. "Damn, I swore I left it here last night. Maybe Webber took it. That guy's so gung-ho, he makes me nervous."

Dana closed her eyes briefly to summon patience, then tapped him on the shoulder. Hard. "Mulder, pay attention."

"What? What?" He didn't look around. "Maybe I filed it." He shuddered. "God, what a thought."

"It doesn't matter."

"Of course it matters. Do you think I'd actually . . ." He fell silent and slowly turned to look at her. "You have news."

With a look to the ceiling, she thought *thank you* before pushing a hand absently at her hair. "In the first place, I do not appreciate your leaving me alone with that human octopus. I swear to God he has hands growing out of his ears."

At least he had the grace to look contrite. "Sorry. Douglas had the appointment already set up. I had no choice."

When she heard what the Section Head had to say, she told him she had already been briefed. The man had caught her in the hall on the way to Mulder's office.

"But that doesn't make any difference right now."

He was startled. "What do you mean?"

"Table that for a minute. What I want from you now is your word that you'll never, ever leave me alone with that reporter again." She shuddered to prove her point. "I am a doctor, Mulder. I know secret doctor things. If I'm forced to, if he lays one more paw on me, I swear I'm going to make sure he never touches another woman again."

Mulder held up a hand. "Okay, okay. I didn't think he'd be that bad. Honest." He frowned. "I guess this thing about his cousin's boyfriend shook him up more than I thought."

Angrily she told him that was no excuse. It was perhaps understandable, but it was still no excuse. When he apologized again, she allowed herself a moment to calm down, then took the other chair and hauled her briefcase onto her lap.

"What's the other news?" he wanted to know, eyeing the case suspiciously.

"Good news and bad news, actually."

He stared at her for so long, she thought he hadn't heard. Then he slumped a little in resignation and gave her his full attention.

"The good news is, you don't have to go to Louisiana. You can't find the file because Bette took it back just a few minutes ago."

He barely reacted, little more than a blink.

"The other good news is, you're still stuck with me."

A lopsided smile flared and vanished. "The bad news is," he said dryly, "we're going to North Dakota, no bathrooms, and we have to live in a tent."

"Not quite." If it wasn't so infuriating, this whole thing would have been laughable. "Actually, it's New Jersey."

"What?"

She looked up without raising her head. "New Jersey."

He frowned his puzzlement. "Why New Jersey? What—" His eyes widened in dismay. "Oh, God, Scully, please, not the Invisible Man."

She unsnapped the briefcase flaps and pulled out a folder marked with a red tab, set the case on the floor and the folder on her lap. She flipped it open and picked up the top sheet. Only then did she nod, and waited patiently until he had stopped muttering to himself and grunted for her to continue.

"The—"

"Hold it," he said. "Wait a minute. What changed the mighty Douglas's mind? Yesterday it was disappearing clowns, today it's Claude Rains. I don't get it. Does he really think this is an X-File?"

Scully smiled. "I don't know. But it seems your friend has a friend."

"Carl? The sports reporter Carl?" He didn't believe it. "Carl Barelli has friends in high places?" He shook his head slowly; wonders never ceased.

"Not quite," she admitted. "Angie Tonero, his cousin, has a brother. The one who tried to dismember her soon-to-be boyfriend, remember? The brother's name is Major Joseph Tonero. Air Force. Temporarily attached to Medical. You'll never guess where he's currently stationed."

Mulder didn't bother. His expression was enough; he knew that McGuire Air Force Base was adjacent to Fort Dix. "And Major Tonero is . . . ?"

"Apparently, a very good, dear, close personal friend of the Garden State's junior United States senator, John Carmen."

Mulder clearly couldn't decide whether to be amused or angry, and at the moment she wasn't inclined to give him a hand. She only nodded when he said, "Whose office just happened to call the Director, right? Probably in the middle of the night. Probably causing the Director to be not all that happy, which means that when he called the mighty Douglas, our supposedly temporary Section Head lost a lot of sleep. Which, I suppose, means he's really pissed off."

"To put it mildly." She fussed with her skirt, her hair again. "Now, granted, we're not supposed to be at the beck and call of individual members of Congress, but there are budgets and there are appropriations. And the senator is a ranking member of a couple of pretty important committees."

"I love this town," Mulder groused.

She handed over the paper. "This is the report on Frank Ulman."

He took it; he didn't look at it until she stared him into it. When he was finished, no more than a cursory glance at best, she handed him the second one.

"So what's this?" he asked, barely giving it a glance as well. "A second opinion or something?"

"No. And if you'd just look instead of griping . . ."

He did as he was told as he gave her his best

martyr's sigh, and she only just managed not to laugh when he sat up so quickly he nearly slid off the chair. "Scully . . ." He read the papers carefully, one hand pushing through his hair.

"Right," she said. "Two killings. One week apart. Saturday night, early Sunday morning. Each victim with a slashed throat, no other injuries, no indication of robbery or sexual assault. That wouldn't necessarily make them connected, except for the fact that now it seems there was a witness to the first murder too."

Mulder's lips moved as he read the second sheet more carefully. "Another Invisible Man?"

"Could be."

"Or the same one."

"Could be."

"This first guy"—he checked the report— "Pierce, he was drunk. So was the witness."

"No question."

He compared the reports again. "And the second witness, to Frank's murder, she was drunk, too. And . . . drugs?"

"That's right. Heroin."

She saw the look, saw the slight quickening of his movements.

"So . . ." He closed one eye, and his lips twitched into a faint smile. "So . . . maybe."

"Could be."

"Scully," he said, "I give up, all right? You've made your point about Barelli. Several times, in fact." He reached for the folder.

She shook her head. "Not yet."

The frown returned. "What is this? I'm being tortured because I wouldn't look at the slides of your trip? You want me to personally break Carl's arms?"

"No. It's just that there's . . . well . . . a tad more bad news."

"Tad?" He leaned forward. "You just said tad?"

"Hank, actually."

It took him a moment to figure it out, and dismiss it with a *no big deal, we can live with it* wave.

"And company," she added.

Someone knocked on the doorframe.

"What the hell does that mean, 'and company'?" he snapped. "Scully, what's going on, huh?"

She stood, pointed to the door, and said, "Fox Mulder, meet the company."

"Hi," said the tall blonde entering the office as Mulder stumbled to his feet. "I'm Licia Andrews. I'm really glad to meet you, Agent Mulder. Hank's told me so much about you."

"Hank?" Mulder echoed dumbly as he shook her hand.

Licia glanced at Dana. "Why, yes. Hank Webber. Didn't he tell you? We're partners. Sort of. We're going to New Jersey with you. Right, Agent Scully?"

"Oh, yes," Dana said, enjoying herself immensely, and not the least bit ashamed of it. "Absolutely."

● ● ●

The view from the apex of the Delaware Memorial Bridge was probably spectacular—the Delaware Bay below, wooded shoreline upriver, the ocean to the right, the factories and plants that lined the banks on both sides. It probably was, but Barelli never saw it. He hated the height, hated the seagulls gloating at him from eye level, and his knuckles bled white every time he crossed it. Still, it was better than flying by a factor of ten.

And once on the north side, he aimed his battered yellow Taurus straight for the Turnpike, not wasting any time. Despite the call he had made even before he had seen Mulder, and despite the senator's reassurances that the family matter would be expedited, he didn't quite believe it.

Especially after what Dana had said.

After refusing, again, to succumb to his charms, she had coldly walked him to the hushed, vast lobby and had, for God's sake, patted his goddamn arm as if he were a kid.

"Stick to sports, Carl," she'd said. "I'm sorry about the corporal, but use your head, okay?"

He'd been so mad, he'd barely been able to kiss and hug her goodbye.

Stick to sports.

Who the hell did she think she was, Sherlock Holmes in a skirt?

Besides, he was not a sports reporter. He was a reporter whose interests happened to lie in sports. There was a difference, and he was going to prove it.

Fifteen minutes later he was speeding north on the Turnpike, through a speckled twilight rapidly slipping into dusk, ignoring the press of the forest on either side, or the late-hunting hawks that drifted patiently above the dense scrub oak and twisted pine that made up the Pine Barrens. He ignored the speed limit as well, keeping to the left of the two lanes, pushing seventy. The Yankees on the radio. Wind from the open passenger window stirring scraps of paper and crumpled tissues on the back seat and floor. A cigarette in his left hand.

Goddamn bitch. He wondered why he wasted his time, and smiled mirthlessly at the all too obvious answer—she wouldn't give in. He admired that. Hell, he admired her. And one of these days she would learn to admire him.

Soon.

It would be soon.

Although he wasn't exactly a national figure, his byline in this state carried with it no little recognition. He figured he could trade on that once he reached Marville, wherever the hell that was. It sounded like, and most likely was, a two-bit town that leeched off Fort Dix and McGuire. A celebrity like him should find loose tongues easily. A few drinks, a few questions, a few slaps on the back and a couple of knowing winks, and effing Fox Mulder could kiss this reporter's ass.

Besides which, Ulman had practically been family. The last time he had seen Angie, her eyes had been so puffed from crying she could barely see.

Nobody, but nobody, did that to his people.

In fact, with a little luck, he might catch the creep alone, the one who did Frankie in.

He smiled again as he switched on his head-lamps.

The smile didn't last.

He couldn't hold it.

All he could hold was the steering wheel, and the idea that Carl Barelli wasn't going to be deterred by some freak with a knife. He knew others saw him as soft, too long at the desk. Too often for them, those others found out different.

Don't worry, Angie, he promised to the early night; *you hang in there, kid, Cousin Carl is on the job.*

Dana had never liked the way moonlight and headlight bleached the land of its color. There was never any real white, only black and shades of grey, and the things that moved between them.

Graveyard time.

She reached for her left ear and pinched the lobe, just sharply enough to hurt and wake her up. She had thought, had hoped, she would be done with long-distance driving for a while, but Mulder had insisted there was no sense waiting until tomorrow. They might as well get their act together and the show on the road so they'd be ready to work first thing Friday morning.

That wasn't so bad, actually. He had volunteered to do all the driving, brought the coffee and some sandwiches, and had somehow convinced Webber that he ought to drive on alone with Andrews, get to know her, let her get to know him. Partners, he had lectured solemnly and truthfully, had to be able to predict each other's reactions so backs could be guarded and missteps minimized when the action got hot. What he had failed to tell them was that the action hardly ever got hot, except in the movies.

Unless, of course, the partner was Fox Mulder.

Licia hadn't minded; Webber, to Scully's amazement, had actually seemed flustered.

Now she figured them to be fifteen minutes ahead, their first assignment to book rooms in a motel called the Royal Baron, a recommendation Mulder had picked up from a visiting agent stationed in Philadelphia.

There was no question it would be as horrid as it sounded. Mulder was an expert at picking such places. He called it a knack; she knew it was a curse.

"You okay?" He glanced over. "You can sleep if you want."

"Mulder, it isn't even nine. If I sleep now, I'll be awake at dawn." She watched him for a moment, then reached over and turned down the heater. The night was chilly, but it wasn't that cold. "What's the matter?"

He shrugged. "Nothing."

"This breaking into pairs isn't your style."

"Maybe, but four agents driving into a place

called Marville would be like a parade, don't you think?"

"And two cars with agents isn't?"

He said nothing.

A mile passed, black and grey, before she repeated her earlier question. "And don't jive me, Mulder, I'm not in the mood."

He laughed silently. "Good lord. First 'tad,' now 'jive.' What the hell did you do on that vacation?"

"I didn't change the subject every time I was asked a question."

He drove on, thumb tapping lightly on the wheel. "I had a visitor the other day."

She listened as he told her about the man at the Jefferson Memorial, not saying a word. At one point she pulled her coat closer across her neck; when he had finished she had folded her arms across her stomach. She didn't doubt that the meeting had occurred, but she had never been able to fully accept his absolute belief in extraterrestrial life, or his notion that there were those in the government, and those seemingly beyond the government's reach, who were just as convinced, and were as dangerous to him as any murderer they had ever sought.

Add to that the equally bizarre idea that among those Shadow People, as he called them, there were also a handful who were actually on his side, and in any other human being she would see a full-blown case of whatever lay beyond extreme paranoia.

In Mulder, however, it almost seemed plausible.

All right, she admitted; maybe more than "almost."

The Tweed Man, on the other hand, was more likely a coincidence, nothing more, and when she said so, he only grunted. Not entirely convinced, but with no solid reason to think otherwise.

"So what does this case mean to . . . whoever?" she said, staring out at the dark by her shoulder. "And what does it have to do with Louisiana?"

"Beats me. I'm not a psychic."

She shifted. "Mulder, weird stuff, remember?"

He tapped his forehead. "Got it stapled right here."

She caught the grin and held her silence until the silence made her sleepy. Then: "So what does it mean to you?"

"I don't know. Well, yes, I do. It means we have two people dead, and there'll probably be more." A glance, a quick smile. "That's all, Scully, that's all."

She nodded her approval, even though she knew there was no question he was lying.

SEVEN

The Royal Baron Motel was a long, white and red, two-story stucco building facing the two-lane county road that led into Marville. On the west side was the office, whose spot-lighted top was supposedly a bejeweled gold crown; on the east was a restaurant; between them were two dozen rooms, twelve up and twelve down, with a red iron stairway in the center and at each end.

Behind it, and across the road, there was nothing but dense forest.

The restaurant—booths along the windows, round tables at the far end, and a long counter—was called the Queen's Inn.

Exhausted, Mulder slumped by the window

in a red leatherette booth, still feeling as if he were on something that moved and had no intention of stopping. His head throbbed, his vision blurred now and then, and all he really wanted was to crawl into bed and forget the world existed for a while. Webber and Andrews, however, had been waiting in the office, rooms already booked, just as he and Scully had pulled up. Despite his protestations, he was dragged off for something to eat.

They were the only customers in the room; the young waitress spent her time dusting gleaming tables and whispering to the cook through the serving gap in the back wall.

He didn't order anything—the very thought of food made his stomach lurch—but when the orders arrived, he had to admit that the plate of silver dollar pancakes Webber had in front of him actually smelled pretty good.

"That bacon's going to kill you," Scully said dryly, nodding to the double side order beside Webber's plate.

"My guilty pleasure," Webber told her with a boyish grin, and poured what Mulder figured was at least a gallon of syrup over the heavily buttered stack.

Scully watched in amazement. "Never mind."

Andrews had contented herself with a cup of soup, her lean face etched with weariness, her topcoat buttoned all the way to her chin.

Outside the window, a breeze danced with a handful of dead leaves, guiding them onto the road where they were scattered by a passing car.

"So are we going to check it out tonight?" Webber wanted to know.

Mulder looked at him blankly. "What?"

The agent pointed over Mulder's shoulder with his loaded fork, then yanked it back when syrup began to drip on the table. "Marville. Are we going to check it out tonight?"

He shook his head. "Not until morning. Then the first thing we have to do is introduce ourselves to the local chief, let him know we're here."

Webber nodded. "Hawks."

Mulder blinked.

"Hawks," Webber repeated. "Todd Hawks. The Chief of Police. That's who he is."

"Ah."

Webber glanced at his partner, but her attention was on the empty road, and stifling a fierce yawn with her hand. "Didn't you read the file? I mean, it's all in there. About him. Hawks, I mean."

A gust shimmered the window.

Andrews shivered, but she didn't look away.

"Fox?"

"Mulder." He pushed a hand back through his hair. "Don't call me Fox. Mulder is fine."

Webber nodded once, correction noted and filed, it won't happen again.

This kid, Mulder thought wearily, is going to drive me up the wall.

And since he knows the drill full well, he must either be too excited, too eager, or he's scared. That wouldn't be surprising. So far, the young man's field work had been primarily confined to the immediate DC area. Now he was out here, no convenient home office to run to, working with a guy supposed to be more than a little off-center.

That almost, but not quite, made him feel better.

Andrews finished her soup, yawned, and stretched her arms stiffly over her head, clasping her hands and popping her knuckles. "God," she said huskily. "God." The topcoat did nothing to mask her figure.

Mulder felt Scully's shoe poke his ankle, so he figured he must have been staring, even though nothing had registered. That more than anything convinced him it was time to stop being sociable and make his good nights. What he hadn't counted on, however, was Webber trying to save the Bureau a buck by booking only two rooms, one for the ladies, one for the men.

As he unlocked the door and staggered in, tossing his small suitcase on the nearest bed, he said, "If you snore, Hank, I'm going to have to shoot you."

Webber laughed nervously, swore he slept like a baby, and laughed again while he unpacked, toiletries neatly arranged in the bathroom, fresh suit hung on the clothesrack by the bathroom door, the rest put away in the second drawer of a low dresser that stretched halfway along the left-hand wall.

Mulder was too tired to watch the ritual; he'd take care of his own things in the morning. He washed, he undressed, he was in bed and sleeping within ten minutes, ignoring the soft voice of the news on the TV.

He dreamed.

of a room not quite fully dark, outlines of bedroom furniture, outline of a window where the moon crept around the curtains;

a cool night and all the voices that go with it, from soft whispering leaves to the call of tree frogs and crickets;

a faint rumbling, but he knew he didn't live near the tracks, knew it wasn't a train;

louder, and the light around the curtains brightened to a glare, spearing suddenly into the room, shifting, slants and darts stabbing across the walls, the bed and the figure that lay on it, the ceiling, as if its source was spinning slowly outside the window;

frightened

he was frightened, standing by the door, slowly dropping into a crouch;

too frightened to move when the light became too bright and the rumbling too loud and the figure on the bed rose and tossed the coverlet aside, her young face colorless, her young eyes wide not with fear but with intent;

he wanted to stop her, but he couldn't stop dropping, couldn't stop himself from trying to push backward through the wall to get away from the light that exploded into the room, making him scream as the girl child was taken and swallowed by the white.

making him scream.

Making him gasp and sit up, crushing his pillow against his chest, blinking sweat from his eyes, sheet and blanket kicked away from his legs.

When he thought he could move without falling over, he sat on the edge of the mattress and put the pillow against the headboard. A forced shudder, a hard swallow, and he pushed himself to his feet, padding around a cheap table beneath its hanging lamp to the thin drapes on the room's only window. He parted them and looked out, and saw nothing but the road and the trees ranged beyond.

He couldn't see the stars, but he knew they were there.

Behind him, Webber snored lightly.

Oh, boy, he thought; oh, brother.

He wiped his face with a forearm and moved quietly into the bathroom, closed the door, but didn't turn on the light. He knew what he could see—a man forever haunted by the disappearance of his sister, Samantha, when both of them had been children. The dream tried to tell him how.

Maybe it was true, maybe it wasn't. It didn't make any difference.

Dream or not, it was what kept him going.

He splashed water on his face to sluice away the tears he hadn't noticed, before, dried himself, and returned to bed.

He didn't look at his watch, but he didn't think it was much beyond midnight.

A truck rumbled by.

When he slept this time, he didn't think he dreamed.

"Dana?"

Scully grunted to tell Licia she was awake, and to tell her she was also trying her best to get to sleep, whatever it was, it could wait until morning.

"Is there something . . . is there something wrong with Mulder I should know about?"

The voice out of the dark was naturally husky, almost masculine; she had already seen its effect on Webber and Mulder, and wondered how well Licia knew how to use it. It could be a devastating weapon, no question about it. She smiled at the ceiling—*when used for Good, not Evil.*

"Dana?"

She sighed loudly and rolled onto her side. "No. He's fine."

"He sure seemed out of it."

"It's the beginning."

"The what?"

Scully wasn't sure how to explain; after all this time, she barely understood it herself.

"At the start of every case that really catches his attention, he gets . . . hyper. Charged up." To say the least, she added silently. "Then, unfortunately, he has to get where the case is. He doesn't like that, the traveling. In fact, he hates it. It's valuable time wasted when he . . . we could be doing our job. So whenever he gets there, all that initial energy has been expended on the trip. So he crashes."

Silence for a moment before: "Will he be all right in the morning?"

She frowned her puzzlement. Concern was understandable for someone who hadn't worked with Mulder before, but she thought she detected something more in the woman's voice. Her eyes closed, half in a prayer that Andrews wasn't going to screw things up by developing a crush.

"He'll be fine," she answered at last.

"Good."

She said nothing.

The woman's voice faded as she rolled over. "I'd hate to have my first real case screwed all to hell."

Scully almost sat up to demand an explanation and, in the process, an apology. It was natural for someone like Andrews to want to shine first time out. God knows, she had prayed for it herself a hundred times before that first one. In fact, it had made her a nervous wreck. But not only didn't Andrews seem nervous, she seemed almost too calm, too ready. And that could be just as bad.

Or, she thought, I could be overreacting because I'm so damn tired.

A truck growled by.

She yawned, and tucked the covers up under her chin.

"Dana?"

This time Licia's voice sounded very small, very young.

"I'm listening."

"Do you think I'll have to use my gun?"

The corner of her mouth pulled back. "Hardly ever, Licia, believe me."

"Really?"

"Yes." She paused. "The government's too cheap to buy us all that ammunition."

Silence again, while she thought, dear Lord, I'm starting to sound like Mulder.

Then Andrews giggled, laughed, and said, "I guess I've been watching too many movies." The rustle of sheets was followed by, "Good night. And thanks."

"You're welcome, and good night."

Another truck drove by, this one in the opposite direction. Scully listened to the engine until she couldn't hear it anymore, using the fading grumble to pull her into sleep.

Her last thought was of Mulder.

She hoped he wasn't dreaming.

EIGHT

The blue of the previous day turned to thickening overcast shortly after Friday's dawn. By the time Mulder and his team were on the road, Webber driving, a chill easterly wind had begun to coast down the road, sweeping leaves and brown pine needles in front of the car.

Mulder didn't like it; it looked too much like late autumn.

Marville itself began a quarter of a mile from the motel, with a handful of houses squatting in clearings hacked out of the Barrens on either side of the road. Sandy, pebbled soil served as shoulders, and showed as bare spots on lawns looking as tired as the houses themselves.

He sensed right away the little town was dying.

The commercial district was five short blocks long, some of the businesses spilling around the corners. None of the buildings were more than three stories tall, mostly wood, a few with weather-stained stone or brick facades. He counted six that were for rent, and far too many whose display windows had been boarded up with plywood or painted a dead white. A narrow banner sagged over Main Street, announcing the community's 150th anniversary, which made him wonder, as he often did, what had caused this place to attract settlers in the beginning. There was no river, the trees weren't lumber quality, and Fort Dix hadn't been established until 1917, neighboring McGuire Air Force Base some time later.

Webber snapped his fingers, and jerked a thumb to his left. "Barney's Tavern."

Mulder spotted the corner bar, one of several still operating on the street, and supposed that, whatever the reason for Marville's founding, its eventual life support must have been traffic from the post and Air Force base. And solid support as well, from the looks of things. He could see, behind the faded paint and needed repairs, a town that had done quite well for the time that it had had, especially considering what must have been the fierce competition from other towns around it.

A stolid granite bank anchored the next corner, on the left. The shops here were still very much in business, or as much as they were going to get with the economy the way it was, and the Army post drastically cut back over the past several years.

"This is depressing," Andrews said from the back seat. "How could anyone live here?"

"Cheap housing, for one thing," Webber supposed, slowing to allow a trio of old women to make their way across the street. "It's not near very much. I remember the map, but I don't think you can commute all the way to Philadelphia from here easily. Not and make any money."

Inertia, Mulder suspected, was the rest of the answer. No place to go when you can barely afford to live here. Anyone asked would probably give a different answer, but it no doubt boiled down to, "Why bother?"

"There," Scully said, the first time she'd spoken since breakfast.

A single-story, long white clapboard building took a third of the block on the right. A new, gold-lettered sign in front marked it as the police station; an American flag drooped from a flagpole next to the double-door entrance.

Webber pulled into a space in front, rubbed his hands eagerly, and fairly leapt from the car, hustling around to open the rear door for Andrews.

Mulder moved more deliberately, waiting

until Scully joined him. They didn't speak, just exchanged quick *are you ready* glances and started up the concrete walk. Andrews wanted to know why they had to start here since the senator's connections were with Fort Dix and the Air Force.

Scully averted her face from a mild gust. "Let's just say it's usually a little easier dealing with civilians."

"Their loss," said Webber brightly.

Mulder looked at him, looked at Scully, and pulled open the door, allowing the others to proceed him into an open room that took up the entire front third of the building. A waist-high wood rail stretched from wall to wall, and just left of its center gate a uniformed dispatcher sat at her radio, scribbling in a logbook; behind her were three metal desks, none of which were occupied.

To the gate's right a fourth, much larger desk faced the entrance. Behind it was a policeman whose uniform, Mulder reckoned, had been tailored for him ten years and twenty pounds ago. His face belonged to a man who spent most of his time outdoors, and a lot of that time drinking. His hair was brush-cut, and at one time had been red.

Mulder took out his wallet and held up his ID. "FBI, Sergeant, good morning." He spoke politely, with well-practiced due deference. He introduced the others quickly. "We're here to see Chief Hawks."

Sergeant Nilssen wasn't visibly impressed. He said nothing, just pushed away from his work and took his time walking to an unmarked door in the rear wall. Mulder saw the puzzlement in Webber's expression, the outrage in Andrews's. "It's their turf," he reminded them quietly. "They didn't ask for us, remember?"

"Still," Webber answered.

Mulder had neither the time nor the inclination for a quick lesson on the politics of competing law enforcement agencies. He kept his attention on the sergeant, who stood in the open doorway, one hand on a cocked hip, the other trying to scratch the small of his back, then his nape. Beefy, maybe, but not very soft. A glance at the dispatcher, who stared back at him without apology. She was in her late twenties, evidently enamored of heavy makeup and the way her wavy brown hair puffed down to her shoulders.

When she finally nodded a greeting, he nodded politely back.

"Slow day?" Scully asked her, looking around the empty room.

She shrugged—her name tag read *Vincent*—and waved one hand. "Guys are on the road." A faint smile. "Rush hour, you know?"

Scully chuckled as the woman coughed lightly into a fist.

"Poison ivy?" Mulder said, nodding at the blotches of white lotoin on the back of her hand. "I hate that stuff."

Vincent made a face in agreement. "Yeah, I got it—"

"Hey."

The sergeant beckoned with a crooked finger.

Webber stiffened, but Scully touched his arm as Mulder led the way through the gate, smiling, always smiling, thanking the sergeant as he stepped aside to let the others precede him.

Nilssen didn't smile back. After an expressionless, just shy of openly rude once-over, he returned to his desk, leaving Mulder to make the introductions again, this time to Todd Hawks.

The Marville chief was younger than Mulder expected, not much older than his mid-forties, thick black hair brushed straight back from a widow's peak that pointed at where his heavy eyebrows nearly met across the bridge of a slightly hooked nose. He did not wear a uniform, nor did he wear a tie. White shirt and black trousers, their matching jacket on an antler coat rack in the corner.

His desk was battleship gray, just like the others, the only personal touch a silver-frame triptych Mulder noted held pictures of what must be his wife and three children.

Hawks rose and shook their hands, waving Scully and Andrews to the only other chairs in the room. Webber chose to lean against the wall near the door, arms folded casually across his chest.

The chief picked up a sheet of paper, glanced at it, and frowned. "I have to tell you, Agent

Mulder, this fax your man Webber sent kind of took me by surprise. I wasn't expecting any feds to get involved." He let the paper drop, glanced at the closed door, and fingered a pen in his breast pocket. "To tell you the truth, though, I think I'm glad to see you. This shit's a little deep for me and my people, and those—" He stopped, lowered himself back into his chair and picked up a pencil he rapped on the desktop. "The gentlemen from Dix aren't really much on letting us hick boys in on much of anything, even though the corporal wasn't killed on post." He used the eraser to scratch at his temple. "Technically, the Ulman murder is ours. Try to tell them that, though."

Mulder gave him the perfect *us against them* smile. "That's what we're here for, Chief. We're going to need all the assistance we can get, and we'd definitely appreciate all you can tell us."

"No problem." Hawks, like his sergeant, wasn't awed, but not for the same reasons. "You just let me know what you need, I'll do what I can." The pencil tapped as his expression darkened. "The thing is, I didn't know that corporal at all. Grady Pierce, though, he was a royal pain in the ass, but I could think of a couple dozen guys I'd rather see take it the way he did. The poor son of a bitch."

"Friend of yours?" Webber asked from the back of the room.

Hawks looked around Mulder at him, shaking his head. "Not really, no. Just known him a long time. Retired drill instructor, wife left him right after the service forced him out." He looked back at Mulder. "He had no skills to speak of except bending his elbow, and AC."

Andrews, who had been sitting stiffly in her chair, distaste clear in the set of her lips, said, "AC?"

"Atlantic City, Agent Andrews," the man explained.

"Oh." Distaste became disdain. "Gambling."

Hawks didn't blink; he only nodded.

"So you think it was a gambling debt or something?" Webber asked, dropping his arms, eagerness creeping into his voice. "Pierce, I mean?"

"Not hardly. When he went, he mostly won." He grinned. "Nicely supplemented his retirement pay, which wasn't a hell of a lot." He opened the center drawer and pulled out a folder. "This is pretty much what we've got on both men, Agent Mulder." He handed it over. "You can see it isn't much, even after two weeks with Grady." He shook his head and shrugged. "The trail's probably dead, if you'll excuse the expression. You're welcome to it, though."

Mulder nodded his thanks and handed it to Scully, who flipped through it and frowned. "I don't see any body diagrams in this autopsy report. Just photographs, and not much commentary."

Hawks scowled. "You'll have to ask them on

the post about that. It seems they cared as much about old Grady as we did."

Well, well, Mulder thought. No love lost between Marville and Fort Dix. He wondered if that extended to the merchants as well.

Scully held a sheet of paper closer to her eyes, frowning in confusion. "What's this say here in the margins? Gablin? Goblin?"

Mulder looked at her quickly. "Goblin?"

"Go see Sam Junis," the chief suggested as she slapped the folder shut. "He's the local doc, did the work on both men. He scribbles a lot, half the time nobody can read it but him. He lives in the first house west of where you're staying. He knows you'll be dropping in."

"How did you know where we were staying?" Andrews demanded.

Mulder didn't turn, but he hoped the chief wouldn't take offense.

"Miss," Hawks answered with a lazy smile, "you maybe have noticed we're not exactly the metropolitan Washington area around here. And this time of year, Babs out there at the motel doesn't get hardly any business except on weekends, and not much even then. Hell, if you want, I'll even tell you what you had for breakfast."

"What?" Webber asked, as if the chief were a magician about to reveal an ancient secret.

Hawks looked at Mulder—Is this one for real?—and stood. "You're the redhead, so you had more pancakes than you ought to, gonna need a new notch on that belt, son, before long. Agent Scully had toast and coffee, bran cereal, orange juice. Agent Andrews had tea, toast, corn flakes. And you, Agent Mulder, had toast, bacon, two eggs over medium, coffee, orange juice, and blueberry jam."

Mulder grinned his appreciation as the chief came around the desk and ushered them to the door.

"And I suppose you know what side of the bed I slept on?" Andrews asked coldly.

"Beats the shit out of me, Miss," he said. "Damn drapes were closed too tight."

Mulder couldn't help it; he turned away and laughed as the chief asked them to wait outside while he cleared a couple of things up before taking them down to the first crime scene. Although it looked as if Andrews was about to object, Mulder agreed immediately and shook the man's hand, thanking him again for his cooperation. Then he herded the team into the outer office, nodded to the sergeant—the dispatcher was gone, replaced by a man who stared at them, bewildered—and didn't stop again until he was on the front walk, but unfortunately, not before Andrews made a deliberately loud comment to Hank about the "insufferable hicks in this damn burg." Mulder, hands in his open topcoat pockets, looked up the street, seeking patience and inspiration, and a way to heed Scully's silent warning not to lose his temper.

"Look," he finally told them, "we have to work with these people, you understand? We need them on our side so we can do our job and get back to Washington as quickly as we can. I don't care what you think of them personally," he said to Licia, "but you keep your comments to yourself from now on, understood?"

She hesitated before nodding, and he made a note to have Scully Dutch uncle her later.

Webber, chastened even though he hadn't been the one scolded, cleared his throat. "Uh, Mulder? Who's Babs?"

Mulder nodded toward the far end of town. "Babs Radnor. She's the owner of the motel."

Webber frowned. "How did you know that?"

Without looking at Scully, he said, "Spooky, Hank. I'm just damn spooky," turned and pointed to a brick-faced diner across the street. "We'll meet there about one for lunch, okay?" He told Hank and Andrews to canvass the area around Barney's, talk to everyone they could find about the dead men, the bar's reputation, the night of the murder, anything at all that might yield them information the reports hadn't told them.

Webber almost saluted as he led his partner off, leaning close, whispering urgently.

"Hello," Mulder said quietly as Scully came up beside him. "My name is Agent Webber, FBI. Tell me all you know or I'll smile you to death."

She slapped his arm lightly. "Give him a break, Mulder, okay? He's not all that bad."

He agreed. "But it's not him I'm worried about."

He looked at the sky, at the lowering clouds, and smelled the first hint of rain as the wind strengthened, snapping the tired banner, scattering debris in the gutters. At that moment, nothing moved on the street.

No pedestrians, no cars, not even a stray dog or cat.

"Ghost town," Scully said.

"Graveyard," he answered.

NINE

They walked east along Main Street, Mulder on the outside. The deserted moment had passed, and shoppers, not many, drifted in and out of stores, while automobiles and pickups made their way between the traffic lights. Few bothered to look at him and Scully, and those who did smiled faintly and moved on.

A breeze drifted down the sidewalk, picking up strength, flapping his open topcoat against his legs, slipping an unpleasant chill inside his suit.

Scully followed the meandering progress of a mongrel along the curb. "Did you notice how he changed? Hawks, I mean?"

He nodded. "Cop for us, hick for Licia. The man's no dope. I'm actually a little surprised he didn't ask for help right away. As far as I can tell, when they need a detective, he's it. And what's with Andrews, anyway?"

She shrugged. "First case jitters?"

He supposed it could be, but he didn't like it. Like the assignment of this case, it just didn't feel right. He didn't doubt she was competent; she wouldn't have gotten this far otherwise. Something, however, would have to be done about that superior attitude she had taken in the station. Behavior like that would shut Hawks up faster than a judge's order.

As Barney's slipped by them on the far side, he glanced over and saw, as before, nothing special. A tired bar in a tired town. Pick it up and put it down in Michigan or Oregon, it wouldn't change. And immediately he thought it, he realized he had probably made a big mistake, letting her go with Webber. The man had a knack for getting people to talk to him. That face, that grin, that shock of red hair was disarming. He hoped it would be enough to offset Licia Andrews.

The morning light dimmed.

The scent of rain grew stronger.

From the corner of his vision he watched Scully tracing the probable path Grady Pierce had taken, leaving the bar, making his way at some point across the street, maybe weaving, maybe not. An empty street. Light rain.

"He didn't see anybody," he said as they approached the alley. It was set between a pair of three-story brick buildings, clothing stores on the ground floor in both, what looked to be apartments above.

Scully didn't question him. "Or he didn't notice."

"That late, in this town? On a Saturday night? It may not be very healthy, but it isn't dead yet. He would have noticed. Especially if it was raining."

Again Scully didn't argue. She only said, "Unless he knew him."

A sideways glance: "Sexist comment, Scully. I am offended."

"Impersonal pronoun, Mulder. I am unbiased. So far."

Just as they reached their destination, a gleaming white patrol car pulled in at the curb, facing in the wrong direction. Chief Hawks slid out, jacket and tie in place, hair barely touched by the breeze now a wind. As he came around the trunk, he was greeted by several pedestrians, and he responded in kind, calling each by name. He slipped a hand into a pocket as he joined them, pushing the suit jacket behind his arm.

Mulder saw the shoulder holster.

The chief shivered, rolling his shoulders against the damp. "Are you sure about this?"

"I know it's old," Mulder answered, "but it's always better than reading about it in a report."

"Visualization," Scully added.

Hawks nodded understanding. "So . . . ?"

The alley was a few inches wider than six feet,

extending another twenty yards to a twelve-foot-high, weather-stained stockade fence. Although there were no garbage cans or a Dumpster, there were small fluttering islands of wind-deposited trash against the base of the walls. There were no windows. There were no fire escapes. The yellow crime scene ribbon had long since been taken down.

They stood on the sidewalk, forcing what foot traffic there was to walk behind them.

The stores on either side had SALE signs in their windows, but the one on the right was dark, nothing on display. Above, the windows were all curtained or blind with shades.

Somebody died here, Mulder thought; some poor guy bled to death here.

It was time to walk the crooked path.

Hawks pointed: "Grady was found there, a couple of feet in, sitting against the wall. Even with the rain, it looked like he took a shower in his own blood."

Mulder took a single step in and hunkered down, looking at the spot, looking over and up at the wall. He saw no evidence of the dying, but he could sense it here just the same.

Scully stood behind him. "He was killed where?"

Hawks walked around them and stood about a yard from Mulder. "The way the blood trail was—and again, remember it was raining—it looked like he was cut here, took a step or two, maybe trying to get to the street, and ended up there, where Agent Mulder is." He moved aside when Scully took his place. "The thing is, those streetlights don't reach in very far. A couple of feet at most, and I'll bet he wasn't seeing all that clearly."

"Mulder?"

He rose slowly, watching her turn until her back was against the right-hand wall.

"The killer was standing about here."

Hawks frowned. "How do you know that?"

"The autopsy report," she said, gaze constantly shifting, examining the ground, the opposite wall, the ground again. "If your Doc Junis is right, he'd have to be. Can I borrow your pen?"

The chief, looking for and not getting a reaction from Mulder, handed her a ballpoint, which she held in her right hand as if it were a knife, not for stabbing but for cutting.

"The photographs weren't all that clear," she continued, almost as though she were talking to herself. "But look . . ." She gestured until Hawks stood with his back to the street, then stood in front of him and, before he could move, whipped the pen through the air at his throat.

He jumped.

Her apology was a sardonic smile. "No blood on the walls. It was a single slash, very strong, cutting jugular and carotid. There wouldn't have been a gusher, so to speak, but some significant blood would have hit the walls if he'd been facing in or out." She handed the pen back. "There was none." She pointed in. "And there wasn't any back there, either."

"Rain," the chief reminded her. "And it was at least an hour before he was found."

She nodded. "But the trail, even after all that time, seemed pretty clear, at least from the pictures." She looked up, squinting, using her chin to show the chief the opposing roofs' slight overhang, bulging with sagging copper gutters; it may have been raining, but only a downpour and strong wind would have made the alley as soaked as the street. Then she looked at Mulder. "He was facing the wall."

And that, Mulder knew, was a hell of a thing.

If Scully was right, Grady Pierce would have had to have been damn near blind not to see his attacker.

Unless the attacker was invisible.

"No," she said to the look on his face. "There's another explanation, Mulder."

He didn't respond. He walked carefully, slowly, to the back and poked a finger at the fence. The wood was spongy with rot, and there were no marks on or in it to indicate anyone had climbed over. Or had tried to.

So the killer had left the way he had come in.

"Pierce must have known him," Scully said as he rejoined them.

Hawks agreed. "The way it looks, there's no other reasonable explanation." He sniffed, laughed, hitched at his belt. "Unless you believe Elly."

"The witness," Mulder said.

"If you want to call her that. I wouldn't bet my life on it, though." He led them back to the sidewalk. "See, Elly is what we call in our small town, scientific jargon, a fruitcake." He laughed again, shaking his head. "She's a dear, Elly Lang is, but she has this theory."

"Which is?"

"Oh, no. I'm not going to spoil it. This is something you have to hear firsthand."

The first floor apartment was nearly as dark as the approaching storm.

A single lamp with a saffron chimney on a tilted end table lit only that part of the love seat where Elly Lang sat. Hawks stood in the living room entrance, his back to the tiny foyer; he leaned casually against the wall, hands loose in his pockets. Scully sat in a Queen Ann wingback that smelled of must and mildew. Mulder was on a padded footstool, leaning forward, hands clasped on his knees.

A small room, a Pullman kitchenette at the end of a short hall, a bathroom, a bedroom barely large enough for the single bed and a dresser missing two of its five drawers. Framed prints on the papered walls; a false fireplace with no logs; a jumbled collection of plastic and ceramic horses on the mantel; a fringed carpet worn through in places, only the ghosts of its original colors left behind. The bay window was covered with yellowed flocked curtains tattered along the edges and at the bottom. No television; only a small, portable clock radio on the end table beneath the lamp.

Elly Lang wore discolored, thick-soled nurse's shoes, argyle socks rolled down to midshin, and a simple brown dress without a belt or trim. There was no telling how old she was. In the lamplight she could have been ancient—no lower teeth, collapsed cheeks, strings of dirty white hair untrapped by a hair net. No makeup at all. She kept her hands primly folded in her lap, no rings or watch.

But Mulder watched her eyes. They weren't old at all, and of an odd pale grey that made them appear almost transparent.

"Goblin," she said with a sharp nod, and a *don't you dare contradict me* glare at the chief.

Mulder nodded. "Okay."

She closed one eye partway as she regarded him suspiciously. "I said goblin."

He nodded again. "Okay."

"They live in the woods, you know." Her voice was low, harsh, the rasp of a childhood Halloween witch. "Came when the army did, back in '16, '17, I don't remember, just before I was born." She straightened her spine, and she faded, leaving only the shine of her eyes, the bloodless line of her lips. "Things happen sometimes, and they don't like it."

"What things?" he asked patiently.

"I wouldn't know. I ain't a goblin."

He smiled, just barely, and just barely, she smiled back.

"Miss Lang—"

"Ms.," she instructed. "I ain't blind. I read the papers."

"I'm sorry. *Ms*. Lang. What my partner and I need to know is what you saw that night. The night Grady Pierce died."

"Profanity," she answered without hesitation.

He waited, head tilted, watching her eyes, watching her lips.

"A profane man was Grady Pierce. Every other word out of his mouth a profanity. Especially when he was drinking. Which"—her lips pursed in disapproval—"he was most of the time. Always going on about his ghosts, his stupid ghosts. Like he was the only one in the world who saw them." A slow disapproving shake of her head. "He never listened to me, you know. I told him once, I told him a hundred times to stay home when the goblins were out, but he never listened. Never."

Quietly, respectfully: "You were out?"

"Of course. My obligations, you know."

Mulder questioned her with a look.

"I mark them," she explained. "The goblins. When I see them, I mark them, so this so-called policeman can lock them away until they burn up in the sun. But he never does, you know." The head turned, and Mulder sensed another glare. "He could have saved that old coot's life if he had picked up the marked ones."

"I have a feeling that will change, Ms. Lang," Scully said.

"Damn right it will," the old woman snapped.

"What you saw," Mulder prompted softly.

She shifted, pushing back into the love seat. Her fingers began an endless weaving.

"I was heading home."

"From?"

"The Company G."

Mulder kept his expression neutral. "And that's . . . a bar?"

"A cocktail lounge and restaurant, young man, use the brains God gave you. I do not go to bars. Never have, never will."

"Sorry. Of course."

"It's east of that hideous place Grady always went to, whores and old men, that's all that's there. Around the corner, on Marchant Street. A very nice establishment." The lips smiled. "I know the owner personally."

He heard the chief shift impatiently, heard a faint rustle as Scully shifted in her chair.

Elly cleared her throat to recapture his attention. "I saw Grady up ahead, going into that alley between McConnell's and The Orion Shop. The Orion Shop is closed, you know. They cheated on your change. And the clothes they sold weren't fit for a cow. The goblins drove them away. They do that sometimes, drive the robbers away."

The fingers weaving.

The patter of light rain against the windows.

"I didn't care, of course. About Grady, I mean. He called me names all the time, drunk and sober, so I didn't care at all when he went into the alley. I kept on walking, didn't dare stop, it isn't safe for a woman on the streets at night these days, you know." She looked over to Scully, who nodded her agreement. "I heard a voice."

"From across the street?"

"He was yelling, young man. Grady Pierce always yelled. The army did that to him, made him deaf, I think, so he was always yelling even when he wasn't, if you know what I mean."

Mulder looked at the carpet. "Did you hear what he said?"

She sniffed. "I don't pay attention to things that don't concern me. He was yelling, that's all. I just kept walking."

Fingers weaving, then abruptly still.

He watched her left heel rise and fall, silently tapping.

"I looked over. Natural curiosity, to see what a drunk was yelling at in an alley."

He watched her hands clasp, in a grip so tight he thought the bones might snap. He wanted to cover them, calm them, but he didn't dare move.

"I couldn't see him, except one leg kind of sticking into the light. I saw the goblin, though."

"You did."

The heel stopped; the fingers unwound.

"You don't have to humor me, Mr. Mulder. I don't like being humored. The goblin stepped out of the wall, kicked that old man's leg, and ran up the street."

"Did you call the police?"

She snorted. "Of course not. I knew what they would say. Don't need to be locked up again, not at my age. I'm going to die right here in this house, not in any damn cell."

He gave her that smile again. "But you did call later, didn't you?"

She leaned farther back, all her face now in shadow. "Yes. Yes, I did. Damn conscience wouldn't leave me be until I did, even though I knew they wouldn't do anything about the goblin."

"Ms. Lang?" It was Scully.

Mulder sat up carefully.

"Ms. Lang, what did the goblin look like?"

"It was black, child," Elly said.

"You mean—"

"No, not a Negro, that's not what I mean. I mean just what I said. It was black. All black. It had no color at all."

They stood on the sidewalk outside the building. A handful of children played noisy baseball in a small park diagonally across the street. The brief rain had stopped, leaving behind the clouds, and the smell of wet tarmac.

Hawks seemed embarrassed. "She drinks," he said quietly. "Like a fish. That's all she does when she's not marking her goblins." The laugh he uttered was partly embarrassment, partly mirth. "Orange spray paint, if you can believe it. Most of the time she sits over there in the park, watches the kids play ball. That bench there on the grass by the third base line, that's hers. But every so often she goes off on a tear, I have no idea what triggers it. She starts walking around town, zapping people with orange spray paint. Then she comes to the station and tells me to lock the goblins up."

He waited until they were in the patrol car before he jammed a toothpick into his mouth and pulled away from the curb. "Just about everyone knows her, see, so we don't arrest her or anything. We pay for the clothes or whatever she wrecks, and that's usually the end of it. No real harm done." He grinned around the toothpick. "What you might call local color."

"So you don't think she saw anything?" Mulder asked from the back seat.

"I wish I knew, I really do. We looked, of course, but we didn't find a thing. Myself, I think she saw shadows, that's all. It was raining, there was wind . . . that's all."

No one spoke as he headed back to the station. "But what," Scully asked, "if she did see something?"

The toothpick flipped from one corner of his mouth to the other. "A black goblin, Agent Scully? What the hell am I supposed to do with that?" He didn't wait for an answer. "Like I said, she was drunk, like always, and it was shadows."

Maybe, Mulder thought; but wherever there's a shadow, there's always something to make it.

Then Scully said, "Is she the only one, Chief?"

Mulder saw him twitch.

"Only one what?"

"Is she the only one who's seen the goblin?"

They passed another small park where a pick-up baseball game had drawn a small crowd.

"No," he admitted quietly. "No, damnit, there've been others."

TEN

Major Joseph Tonero loved his sister, even if she did have appalling taste in men. With their father gone and their mother an invalid, he had automatically assumed the role of head of the family. He didn't mind at all. It was not unlike his role in the service, mediating crises between people who were grown up enough to know better, issuing orders carefully couched as strong suggestion, and laying plans for the time when he could trade his uniform for a well-tailored suit that would fit right in on Capital Hill.

So he wasn't all that concerned with the fit Rosemary Elkhart threw in his office in Walson Hospital. He simply sat back, folded his hands in his lap, and let her rant, pacing the oak-paneled room until she finally dropped into an armchair. Her lab coat fell away when she crossed her legs, and he made no effort not to stare.

It wasn't as if he hadn't seen those thighs before.

"So what you're saying," he told her mildly, "is that you're annoyed."

She glowered, but couldn't hold it, finally laughing and shaking her head. "You amaze me, Joseph. You absolutely amaze me."

"Why?"

She sputtered, blinked, slapped in frustration at her bangs. "All that's at stake, and you, of all people, actually call in the FBI. Leonard's thinking about running to Brazil."

The smile he gave her carried no artifice. It wasn't necessary here; she knew all the tricks of his trade, and had taught him a few new ones herself. "I didn't exactly call them personally."

Close enough, her expression told him.

He waved her objection away. "I'm not worried about the feds, Rosie, and neither should you be. They come in, they read the reports, they look at a crime scene that's been cold for a week—"

"And what about Kuyser? She's a witness."

"Oh, really?"

Rosemary shrugged a minor concession. "Okay, not much of one, granted." She toyed with the edge of her coat, just above the knee. "But what about Leonard?"

His expression hardened. "We need him. I don't

like it, you don't like it, but the Project needs him." He rose and walked around the desk, stood behind her and stared blindly at the wall while he massaged her shoulders. "Once this little problem—"

She barked a laugh.

"—is settled, once you're back in the groove, then we'll see about Dr. Tymons."

She tilted her head and kissed his hand. "I can do it, you know, Joseph. It's not hopeless."

"I have every faith in you, Rosie."

"A small adjustment, that's all."

"As I knew it would be."

She turned to look up at him. "A week, perhaps two."

His gaze shifted to her face, that back of his left hand to her cheek, gliding down across her chin. "And . . . confinement?"

She leaned into the hand, eyes partly closed. If she had been a cat, he thought, she'd be purring.

"None."

The hand stopped.

"We can't, Joseph," she said, easing out of the chair. "We have to trust Leonard's judgment on this."

"We already have. Twice."

"If we confine, we lose."

He sighed without a sound. He knew that, yet it was so untidy, so uncontrolled. But if the Project was to work, if the Department of Defense was to be convinced, it wouldn't do to have a psychotic subject. He had little choice. Tymons would continue to be the control until perfection was achieved.

Unless . . .

He took her hand and led her to the door. "Rosie, if there's another failure, I don't think I'll be able to protect him."

Her smile was genuine as well, and he suppressed a shudder when he saw it. "You won't have to, Joseph."

She kissed him quickly and left, the smell of her, the taste of her, lingering in the office. He savored it for a few seconds before striding back to his desk. The problem with Tymons and the Project was the least of his worries right now. He didn't much care if the subject wiped out half the goddamn state; with the right slant, a well-chosen word, it would only prove the Project's ultimate worth. And he had been telling Rosie the truth—his concern over the FBI was minimal as well.

The real problem was that asshole Carl Barelli. The idiot had already called him twice this morning, demanding an appointment, and the major knew well that kind of man—if no appointment was forthcoming, he'd show up on the post anyway and make enough noise to wake the dead.

Not to mention alerting those whose need to know did not, by any stretch of the regulations or imagination, extend to the Tymons Project.

You don't turn on a spotlight when you're working in the dark.

That was the problem with goddamn reporters these days—they thought they owned the goddamn Constitution. Barelli would have to be mollified. Having the FBI around would help. So would assurances that he himself was personally monitoring the situation, maintaining constant contact with the CID and the civil authorities. He'd do that anyway; he wasn't a fool. The fact that he had thought Ulman was a class-A jerk shouldn't deter him from extending what comfort he could to his sister.

Still, if Angie took up with a serviceman again, he would personally see to it the jerk was transferred to South Korea.

He took his chair and reached for the telephone, his free hand drumming thoughtfully on the desk. He would get hold of Carl, meet him for a late lunch, take him on the two-bit tour, pat him on the back, shed a tear with him for the loss of Angie's love, and get the sonofabitch the hell off his post. Let him go back to writing about hockey or basketball or whatever the hell it was he wrote about in April.

Hell's bells, he was only a cousin, for Christ's sake.

It wasn't like he was real family.

Goblins, Elly thought nervously; the goblins are back.

She stood in the kitchenette, squinting

myopically at a calendar hanging on the refrigerator door. She knew those government people hadn't believed her, nobody did, but tomorrow was Saturday again, and the goblins would be back.

She was tired of being the only one who saw them.

That young man, though, he might be persuaded. He had the look about him. The believing look. The wanting look. All she had to do was mark one and show it to him.

That's all it would take.

Once he knew, the others would come around.

She licked her lips and turned to the cupboard under a rust-stained sink. From it she pulled a brand new can of marking magic, shook it, took off the rounded top, and tested it in the sink.

It worked.

She cackled.

Her pale eyes hardened to steel gray.

"So when he took off for California," said Babs Radnor, a distinct Tennessee drawl in her voice, "I got a lawyer, emptied the bank account, took over the motel, and have become, as you can see, a lady of leisure."

She sat in her king-size four-poster, two pillows fluffed behind her back. She bordered on the painfully thin, with short black hair brushed

behind her ears, hard black eyes, and a voice that
husked with too much liquor, too many cigarettes.
Her right hand held a floral sheet modestly over
her breasts, while her left hand held a tumbler of
bourbon and ice.

"I am not a lush, though," she insisted, waving the glass from side to side. "Like the French,
I always have a little something with every
meal. It's supposed to be good for the heart and
circulation."

Carl stood at the low, twelve-drawer dresser
and watched his reflection trying to make sense
of his tie. "That's wine, Babs. Wine."

She shrugged. "Who gives a damn. It's working, right? So who cares?"

He didn't argue. Not even twenty-four hours,
and he already knew she did not take lightly to
contradiction or correction. Nor did she exagger-
ate when she had suggested without being coy or
cute that he would have a much more pleasant
evening in her company than the company of a
TV, even if it did have free HBO.

It beat all to hell paying for a room.

It also afforded him a way to keep tabs on
Mulder and his team. Babs, as she had already
proven, knew everything about every blessed
person who stayed in her motel. And if she didn't
know, she found out. There wasn't, she had con-
fessed, a whole lot else to do around here.

"So anyway, I'm figuring one more year,
maybe two, sell out and get my buns to some-

place like Phoenix, Tucson, someplace like that. Have you ever been to Arizona, sugar?"

He shook his head, damned his tie and yanked it off. He didn't figure the major would take him anyplace fancy anyway. There was, as the saying goes, no love lost between them, and it didn't bother him a bit. Tonero was an ambitious little toad, and Carl's skin crawled each time they met. He didn't know how Angie could be from the same mother. Still, the guy had been sincere enough when they finally connected, and this lunch thing would give him a chance to see where Frankie had died.

Once he had done that, gotten the lay of the land, he could take the next step.

Whatever that might be.

"On the other hand, San Diego is supposed to have perfect weather, you know?" She laughed hoarsely. "The trouble is, it's in California. They hate it when you drink, smoke, and eat a decent meal, a steak and all. I don't know if I could stand it. I'm not too thrilled about those earthquakes, either."

He turned and spread his arms. "So? Do I look good enough to see a major?"

She waggled her heavy eyebrows. "Good enough to eat, if you ask me."

He laughed and sat on the edge of the bed, taking the hand that held the sheet in both of his. The sheet began to slide. "When I'm done, how about I take you out to dinner?"

"Yeah, right."

"Really, Babs, I'd like to. Is there a place around here, someplace nice?"

She looked at him carefully.

The sheet made it to her waist.

"If you don't mind driving a little . . . ?"

His eyes widened comically, showing her his struggle not to look at her chest. "A little?"

"An hour?"

"What's an hour?"

"Atlantic City. There's some really nice places at Resorts and the Taj." Then she stuck her tongue out and laughed, pulled his hands to her breast, and stuck her tongue out again. "Just so you don't forget."

He kissed her then, long and soft. "Like I would," he whispered.

"Liar."

"Maybe." He slipped away and stood. "But I'm damn cute, right?"

She didn't laugh, didn't smile.

He leaned over and kissed her again, quickly but just as earnestly. "See you later."

"I'll be here, sugar. Noplace else to go."

He blew her a kiss from the door, closed it behind him, and hurried down the long gold and royal blue corridor. Her apartment was above the office, tucked behind the crown facade, and he used the outside back stairs to get to his car, hastily parked there when he had spotted that redheaded agent pull up not long after he himself had arrived. He figured he would run into Mulder sooner or later, but right now he preferred it to be later. The way he figured it, the agents wouldn't be here more than a couple of days, not on a case that was as cold as this one, and they'd probably eat at least one meal at the Inn.

They would talk while they ate.

Whatever they said, he would know less than an hour after they were done.

It was so perfect, he crossed his fingers to ward off the feeling that it just might be too perfect.

But he wasn't going to run from it, either. Hell, he got a free room, a free woman, and a chance to sneak up on Dana again. What the hell more could he ask for?

The killer, he answered as he pulled slowly around the side of the building; I want the killer, that's what I want.

He had another feeling, and he leaned forward, looked up, and saw her standing at her bedroom window. He gave her the smile, and the wave, and when she waved back he blew her a kiss before speeding out onto the road.

What a day this was going to be. Lunch with a uniformed toad who thinks his cousin is a jerk, a little investigative work around town, dinner in Atlantic City, a roll in the hay in a bed so big he could build a house on it.

Life, he decided, just doesn't get any better.

Leonard stood at the end of the basement corridor, listening.

He didn't know what he expected to hear. There was never any noise save for the faint grumble of the machines that gave the building its power.

Nevertheless he listened, and wished there were more lights.

A single bulb over the entrance, one down at the far end. Nothing more. No need for more. He and Rosemary were the only ones who used it; Major Tonero was the only one who visited.

Still, he couldn't help thinking there should be some sound other than the rasp of his breathing.

You're making yourself jumpy, he scolded as he started toward the Project office. Not that he shouldn't be. So much had gone right, and so much had gone wrong, that half the time he didn't know whether he should shout or cry. Rosemary didn't help either, nagging at him constantly, pushing him, reminding him unnecessarily that this had to be the right one or all support would vanish as if it had never been.

And, he feared, him with it.

Ten yards down he reached the first of three doors on the right—there were none on the left at all.

The first was his private office. No markings, just dull steel. The second door was the same, the

Project center within. He glanced through the wire-mesh window and saw that it was empty. Rosemary must still be at lunch.

The third door was closed.

He glanced at it nervously, checked back toward the exit, and decided he had to know.

With one hand in his pocket to stop his keys from jangling, he hurried to it and looked through the reinforced glass judas window.

No one sat in the armchair, or at the desk now stripped of everything but the pen and legal pad. He couldn't see the bed.

He flipped a switch by the jamb and rapped lightly on the window with a knuckle, and jumped back with a stifled cry when a face suddenly grinned at him from the other side.

"Jesus," he said, eyes closing briefly. "You scared me to death."

Above the door was a microphone embedded in the concrete, a speaker grille beside it.

"Sorry." The voice was distorted, asexual. "I'm on break. I thought I'd drop in. Sorry."

It wasn't sorry at all.

"How do you feel?" He approached the door again, warily, as if the face belonged to a superhuman monster that could, at the slightest provocation, smash through the steel. The stupid thing was, the door wasn't locked. He could walk right in if he wanted to. If he had the nerve.

"How do you think I feel?"

Tymons refused the bait, the invitation to guilt. That sort of emotion had died the first time he had skinned a subject capuchin alive. He hadn't liked it, of course, but there had been no other way.

Guilt, for the Project, was too damn expensive.

"When do I get to see the results?" It wasn't a plea, it was barely a question.

"Later," he promised. Below the level of the window, he crossed his fingers. Just in case.

"I feel pretty good."

"You're looking good."

He returned the smile.

"I've almost got it, too."

Tymons nodded. He heard that every week, every month. "You'd better. They're . . ." He couldn't help a grin. "They're a little annoyed."

"It wasn't *my* fault. You're the doctor."

He had heard that one, too. Every week. Every month.

"But I'll take care of it."

Tymons glared and pointed. "You'll do no such thing, you understand? You let me handle everything."

The face didn't change expression, but Tymons looked away from the contempt.

"I'd like my books back, please."

He shook his head. "That didn't work, and you know it. The books, the music, the TV. Too many distractions. You need to concentrate on your concentration." He chuckled. "As it were."

"I *can* concentrate, damnit. I concentrate so much my brain is falling out."

Tymons nodded sympathetically. "I know, I know, and I'll talk to you about it later. Right now I have work to do."

Even through the distortion, the sarcasm was clear: "Another little adjustment?"

Tymons didn't answer. He switched off the communication unit, waved vaguely, and hurried to his office. Once inside, he locked the door behind him and dropped behind his desk, switched on his computer, leaned back and closed his eyes.

This was wrong.

Things weren't getting better, and no goddamn adjustments were ever going to work.

He sighed and checked his watch—he had almost two hours before Rosemary arrived. Plenty of time to complete copying his files. Plenty of time to take the Army-issue .45 Tonero had given him and go back next door. And use it.

Plenty of time to vanish.

After all, he thought with a hollow laugh, he was the expert at things like that.

Then he glanced through *The Blue Boy*, and started.

The room was empty.

"Damn." He flicked a switch beneath the shelf, activating the lights embedded in the room's ceiling. All color vanished, all shadows.

Still empty.

GOBLINS

The bastard had already left.

Like a ghost, he thought, glancing nervously at the door; the damn thing moves like a ghost.

After all this time, he couldn't bring himself to think of it as human.

ELEVEN

The overcast thickened, splotches of shifting cloud from grey to black bulging and spreading, using the wind to warn that the rain that had fallen before would be nothing like the rain to come.

Dana stood uneasily in the middle of a narrow paved road, not at all caring for the way the woodland pressed around her, not liking the faint hint of ozone that promised lightning when the storm broke again.

They had eaten in the diner as planned, but neither she nor Mulder had been either surprised or pleased with what they had heard: Webber and Andrews had learned nothing that hadn't been recorded or implied in the reports already. No one had seen anything, no one had heard anything; many of the shopkeepers knew Grady, most of them not kindly; a couple recognized Ulman's picture, but there was nothing more than that. He was from the post. Big deal.

No miracles.

No one had mentioned goblins, either.

Hawks had explained that, over the past couple of months, some kids and a couple of adults had reported seeing . . . something drifting around the town. They called it a goblin because everyone knew of Elly Lang's obsession.

"But it doesn't mean anything," he had insisted calmly. "A story like that, it kind of feeds on itself."

By two, the afternoon light had worsened, shifting closer to false twilight. Mulder decided to check the site of the corporal's murder before the storm broke. Andrews, on a hunch, volunteered to return to the motel to interview the owner; it was possible, she said, Ulman had used the out-of-the-way place for weekend escapes. Maybe he had provoked the wrath of someone's husband. Chief Hawks quickly volunteered to drive and introduce her.

"And keep her out of trouble," Mulder had said later, in the car.

Scully hadn't liked the idea then, and she didn't like it now. Webber, on the trip out, had already told them that Andrews, her attitude unchanged, had made the interviews, brief as they were, "kind of difficult." Except, predictably, when the subjects were men.

Webber stood now some fifty yards up the road, hands in his pockets, playing the part of the Jeep the Ulman witness had been in. He looked miserable as the wind slapped his hair and coat around; about as miserable as she felt.

Mulder was on his third circle of the tree from which the arm and weapon had allegedly appeared. It had been easy to find—there was still a ragged piece of yellow crime scene ribbon wrapped around its thick trunk.

She glanced up; the sky was lower.

Nothing moved in the woods but leaves and bare branches. And the slow-strengthening wind.

Behind her, their car shuddered when a gust slammed it broadside.

She turned in a slow circle, shaking her head. The corporal had been drinking; he had, for some reason, come out of the woods down there by the ditch, staggered up here . . . and had been killed.

Mulder joined her, waving Webber to them. "You see it?" he asked.

The road was a flattened loop that left the county highway just west of Marville, skirted the post boundary here, and met the highway again a mile farther on. While it was possible Grady had been a random victim, there was no way she would believe Ulman had simply been in the wrong place at the wrong time.

The killer had followed him through the woods.

"He was meant to die," she said.

He nodded. "I think so, yes."

Webber trotted up. "So is it hollow or what?"

She frowned. "What? The tree?"

"Sure. That woman saw—"

Scully took his arm gently and turned him around, pointing to the place he'd just left. "There are no lights, there was no moon, and all she saw, from way back there, was whatever the corporal's flashlight showed her."

She waited.

"Okay." He nodded. "Okay. But what was she doing out here?"

Mulder didn't answer. He grunted, and headed back for the tree.

"Well," she said, watching Mulder circle the tree again, squeezing between it and the caged white birch on either side, "she could be an accomplice. She could have been waiting for the killer."

Webber disagreed, as she knew he would. "That would mean they both knew Ulman would be here, at that time. And they didn't, right?"

"Right."

"So it was what? Her bad luck?"

"That's about the size of it," she said. She also reminded them that the so-called witness, Fran Kuyser, had been drinking, and taking heroin. Not exactly the most reliable observer they could hope for.

"When are we going to see her?"

Scully hunched her shoulders briefly. "Later, or tomorrow. From what the chief said, the condition she's in, she won't be able to tell us anything anyway."

"A hell of thing," Webber said. He shifted uneasily. "Can you tell me something?"

She nodded.

"Are the cases you work on . . . I mean, are they always this screwy? Messed up, I mean." He shook his head once, violently. "I mean—"

She laughed in spite of herself. "Yes. Sometimes."

"Brother," he said.

"Tell me about it."

Mulder rapped the trunk with a knuckle, then pried at the overlapping bark. Scully knew, however, that he saw more than just the tree. That was only the center; his focus touched it all.

"That old lady you told me about," Webber said, for some reason keeping his voice low.

Scully didn't look at him. "Ms. Lang. What about her?"

"She said . . . I mean, she was talking about goblins."

She did look then, sharply. "There are no goblins, Hank."

But she knew what he was thinking: She and Mulder were the X-Files, and that meant this case contained something well out of the ordinary. It didn't matter that the so-called paranormal had perfectly reasonable explanations, once you bothered to examine such incidents more closely. It didn't matter that the extraordinary was only the ordinary with curious trappings. They were here, goblins were mentioned, and now she wasn't sure Hank didn't believe it a little himself.

Mulder snagged his coat on a bush, yanked it free angrily, and took it off.

A hoarse cry overhead made her look up—a pair of crows flew lazily across the road, ignoring the wind.

"This place is kind of spooky," Hank said, rolling his shoulders against the damp chill.

She had no argument there. They could see barely a hundred feet into the trees now. If it was twilight out here, it was near midnight in there.

Slipping her hands into her pockets, she called Mulder's name. They would find nothing here; the trail was, for now, too cold.

He didn't hear her.

Goblins, she thought; please, Mulder, don't.

"I'll get him," Hank offered, and was off before she could respond.

He hadn't taken three steps before the first shot was fired.

Immediately, Scully yelled a warning, threw herself around the car and pressed herself hard against the rear fender, gun in hand before she even realized she'd drawn it.

A second shot chipped the tarmac at Hank's

foot, and he cried out, moving backward so rapidly he fell.

Scully eased herself up, squinting into the wind, trying to pinpoint the location of the shooter, knowing only that he was hidden somewhere in the woods east of them. She fired off a quick, blind shot, was answered by a barrage that peppered the road, forcing her back down just as Hank scrambled around the hood and squatted beside her, panting.

"You okay?" she asked.

He nodded, winced, and nodded again.

There was blood on his shoe.

He saw her look and shrugged. "Just a chip from the road on my ankle, that's all." He grinned. "I'll live."

She could see it, he was scared, but she could see the adrenaline, too.

Another barrage, this time at Mulder's position, and she rose again and fired as Hank fired over her head.

Nothing.

She could see nothing.

There was no question it was an automatic weapon, its bark suggesting something less than an Uzi. M-16, maybe. Not that it made much difference now. Bullets slammed into the trunk, walking up to and shattering the rear window.

"Mulder!" she called into the silence that followed.

No answer.

GOBLINS

Hank tugged at her sleeve when the firing paused. "Gas tank," he warned, and on a count of three, they slipped back toward the hood. When the next round was aimed at Mulder, she took the opportunity to dart low across the pebbled verge and into the trees, pressing her shoulder against the trunk of a fat black oak. Webber found a position to her right and deeper into the woods.

"There!" he called, and fired at a point just beyond the far end of the ditch on the other side of the road.

She couldn't see anything, and then—she rubbed a hand quickly across her eyes. In the twisting leaves, a shadow. Or a figure all in black. It didn't move until Hank fired again, and then it vanished.

She looked to her left, and caught her breath.

"He's down!" she called to Webber. "Mulder's down!"

Mulder froze in shocked surprise at the first shot, dropped to the ground at the second, his own weapon out as he heard Scully and Hank return fire. But he couldn't see where the shooter was. The oak, the birch, the underbrush, all blinded him. Quickly, keeping low, he moved to his left, and dropped again when leaves and twigs were shredded above him, peppering his skull, stinging his cheeks.

He covered his head with one arm and

129

waited, moving again when the firing concentrated again on the road, letting instinct take him deeper into the woods, tree to tree, searching for a muzzle flash, firing once, and once again, in hopes of diverting the shooter's attention away from Scully and Webber.

He heard glass shatter.

He heard Scully's voice.

A pine gave him cover, but he flinched anyway when the attack resumed on his original position.

It was luck, then, that the shooter hadn't seen him maneuvering deeper and around, and he used the time to search again, grunting softly when he saw the flash, and a dark figure pressed against the dark trunk of a lightning-blasted tree. He couldn't tell from this distance who it was; the figure had dressed in black from ski mask to shoes.

It didn't look like any goblin to him.

The wind quickened.

He angled inward again, and east, hoping the coming storm's thrashing branches and spinning leaves would make enough noise and present enough distraction that he'd be able to get close enough for a decent shot.

Scully's voice, and Hank's answer; he couldn't tell what they said, but the fear was there.

The black figure backed away, firing.

Mulder cursed and moved more quickly, keeping as low as he could without losing his balance. There were too many shadows now, too much movement.

He had to get there before the shooter disappeared.

At the south edge of a small clearing, he braced himself against a trunk, took several deep breaths to calm down and clear his head, and waited until the firing stopped.

There was no silence.

The wind and the woodland husked and shrieked at each other, pinwheeling debris across the clearing.

He would have to go across it; to go around would waste time.

He inhaled, blew out, and spun away from the tree in a crouch. He was halfway across, aiming, finger already squeezing the trigger, before he realized the shooter was gone.

Damn, he thought, and slowly straightened, not trusting his vision, gun still out and ready, squinting into the wind and throwing up one hand in disgust.

Something moved behind him.

He had only half-turned before something hard slammed off his temple, a glancing blow that drove him to his knees. His gun whipped out of his grip. His right arm lashed out automatically and struck something soft, but he couldn't see clearly; there were too many flares of blinding, painful light.

But he saw something, and it made him hesitate.

Then a blow to his spine almost toppled him, and he lashed out again, losing his balance as he did, landing on his shoulder before he was pinned on his chest.

A giggle in his ear, hoarse and inhuman.

Then a voice: "Mulder, watch your back," just before a foot caught him under his ribs.

TWELVE

He couldn't breathe.

"Mulder!"

Eyes watering, he tried to push himself to his hands, but he couldn't breathe.

"Mulder!"

Forget it, he told his arms, and rolled over instead, blinking furiously to clear his vision, spitting when a shard of leaf caught on his lips.

But he still couldn't breathe.

Voices, normal voices anxious and searching, until his name was called again, and he saw, or thought he saw, Scully kneeling beside him on his left, someone else on his right.

"I don't see any blood," Webber said.

"Mulder?"

He tried to smile reassurance, but it was too much trouble, and he let himself black out, to rest in the dark for a while.

By the time he regained full consciousness, there were sirens and shouts, the distant crackle of a radio. The wind had died, but the afternoon was still night. Scully was gone; Webber hovered nearby, and Mulder groaned to signal him and bring him over.

"Up," he said, stretching out an arm when the younger man leaned down.

"I don't know. Scully said—"

"Up," he insisted, and Webber brought him to his feet.

It was a mistake.

His head swelled to accommodate the fire inside, and he swayed and didn't argue when Webber eased him to a stump at the clearing's north end and made him sit. Bile burned the back of his throat; his stomach surged without delivering. He spat, and spat again, bracing an arm on his leg and resting his forehead on his palm.

"Jesus," he whispered.

Webber hunkered down beside him, concern adding too many years to his face. Mulder glanced over and smiled briefly.

"I'll live."

Webber didn't look as if he believed it. But he told him that an MP patrol, alerted by the gunfire, had arrived only moments after the shooting had stopped. Within minutes, other patrols had arrived, and Scully was advising them and their captain on a search of the woods. When Mulder looked up, he saw silver beams slashing and darting among the trees. Voices called softly. Through the trees he could see half a dozen MP Jeeps and cruisers parked on the road, and a single civilian patrol car, its roof lights still whirling.

"Chief Hawks," Webber confirmed.

Mulder nodded, and wished he hadn't—the fire rose, and fell, and his finger gingerly traced what would be a hell of a lump by nightfall. There was no blood. Then he pushed aside his jacket, opened his shirt, and tried to have a look at his ribs.

"Damn," Webber said. "What'd he use, a brick?"

"It sure felt like it." He winced as he probed the area. He knew nothing was broken, however. How a broken rib felt was something you never forgot.

"Button up, Mulder, you'll catch pneumonia."

He smiled at Scully hurrying toward him. She seemed more annoyed at the wind slapping hair into her eyes than at him.

"You gonna examine me or what?"

"Please," she said. "I've had a bad enough day."

"What happened?" He nodded toward the search party.

"The shooter's gone. No surprise. They found a crushed area back around the bend where he probably stashed his car. No tire tracks, nothing but this." She dug into her pocket and pulled out a casing. "M-16."

"Army?"

"Maybe not," Webber said. "They're not all that hard to get outside the service anymore. Cops, bad guys, collectors." He shrugged. "Even guys leaving the service have smuggled them home."

Mulder muttered about having it easy once in a while. "Well, maybe we should check. How many can there—"

Webber groaned in anticipation. "Mulder, no kidding, it's the weekend. That means there's about eight, nine thousand reservists running all over this place. And you want to find one rifle that's been fired recently?"

"Hank, you amaze me. How did you know that?"

Webber shrugged again. "The interviews, remember? I'll bet the people in town know as much about what's going on on post as anyone who works there."

"Not quite," he muttered. He straightened slowly, hissing at the too-slow lessening pain.

"What I don't get," Scully said, "is how the shooter got to you before we did." Her expression turned sheepish. "I saw your coat on the ground, I thought it was you."

"It wasn't."

"So I see. I don't know what he hit you with,

but he knew what he was doing. He could've cracked your skull wide open." She frowned. "What I don't get is how he managed to change positions so quickly. You were a good—"

"No. I mean, it wasn't the shooter."

She was startled. "What?"

"It wasn't the shooter, Scully. I saw him, the shooter, just before I got hit." He winced as he touched his head again. "From the side, Scully. I was hit from the side, right over there. The shooter was still in front of me."

Doubt was evident in her expression as she put the casing back into her pocket. "The goblin, right?"

"You got it. I just got a glimpse, but believe me, it was enough."

Webber almost laughed, but caught himself when she shook her head in exasperation. "Mulder, you'd just been clobbered, remember? Anything you saw, or thought you saw, would be suspect, you know that."

With Webber's reluctant help, he stood, looking at but not seeing the MPs' shifting lights. "It was a hand, and part of the forearm. The skin looked like bark."

Scully opened her mouth to say something, changed her mind and waited.

"I heard it, too."

She leaned away, an eyebrow cocked. "He left you a message?"

"It was like no voice I've ever heard." He

closed his eyes again, to try to sharpen the memory, felt Webber's fingers lightly on his arm for balance. "I don't know. It was hoarse, whispering, as if it had a hard time saying the words." When he looked, she was scowling, arms folded across her chest. "Honest."

"I don't doubt you heard something. But I—"

"This is a joke, right?" Webber asked nervously. He looked from one to the other. "Some kind of private joke, right?"

Mulder shook his head. "Sorry, Hank, no."

"Oh, man," Webber said, almost in a moan. "Wait 'til Licia hears this one."

Carl Barelli was furious as he sped back through the woods toward Marville.

First, that sanctimonious toad, Tonero, tried to pass off the glop in the Officer's Mess as some kind of fancy food, instead of taking him to a decent restaurant; then tried to hand out some pious bullshit about family unity and Angie's peace of mind being more important than interfering with official investigations; and then he had the nerve to march Carl out to his car and tell him, with a smile, to go on back home and write about baseball or something.

He had fumed behind the wheel, debating the chances of his landing in jail if he went back inside and popped the toad one on the point of his spongy jaw.

Then an MP ran up, intercepted Tonero, and the two were hustled into a car. The next thing Carl knew there were sirens and men with rifles boiling out of the Provost Marshal's office, and, after a suitable interval, he followed them.

To the goddamn woods.

Where another goddamn MP suggested with drawn .45 that the reporter find something else to report on, this area was sealed off to civilians.

"Bastards," he muttered, and muttered it often until suddenly he grinned.

He had seen a town cruiser at the scene, which meant the locals were involved, which meant . . .

He laughed aloud, and by the time he pulled up in front of the police station, his mood had lightened considerably. A quick check of his hair in the rearview mirror, an adjustment of his tie and jacket, and he was inside, smiling at the two men at desks near the back of the room, and the front desk sergeant, who couldn't have looked more bored if he were dead.

"I'd like to see the chief," Carl said, as politely as his excitement would allow.

Sergeant Nilssen told him gruffly the chief was out, and there was no sense hanging around. He had work to do, half his people had some kind of lousy flu, and those who were around had police business to attend to.

A dispatch radio muttered static to itself

while a gawky young officer flipped through a logbook.

Carl's smile didn't waver. "Then perhaps you can help me, Sergeant. I work for the *Jersey Chronicle*. My name is Carl Barelli, and I'm—"

Nilssen's boredom vanished. "Barelli? The sports guy in the paper?"

Amazing, Carl thought smugly; *absolutely amazing.*

"That's right, Sergeant. But today I'm looking into the death of a friend of mine. Corporal Frank Ulman."

"Man, yeah," the sergeant said, grinning. "So you want to hear about the goblins, right?"

The smile still didn't waver. "That's right. Can you help me?"

The policeman leaned back in his chair, hooked his thumbs into his belt. "Anything you want to know, Mr. Barelli. All you have to do is ask."

Tonero remained in the back seat of his staff car, watching as the MPs began to make their way slowly and methodically back toward the road. His driver was gone, ordered to sniff around to see what unofficial word he could pick up. It was better than talking to the captain in charge. Tonero knew the man well, and knew that the MP wouldn't give away a thing.

The car rocked a little when the wind slapped it.

He glanced warily out at what sky he could

see, hoping he'd be able to get out of here before the storm broke.

This was not turning out to be one of his best days. Tymons was jumpy, and Rosemary was getting pushy; and he knew without doubt that Barelli wasn't going to leave until he had gotten some kind of crumb to fill his meager reporter's plate.

He sighed for all the injustices dropped on him since waking, and sighed again when the front passenger door opened and Tymons slipped in at the same time that Rosemary slipped into the back, beside him.

"We heard," Tymons said, agitation making his voice too high.

"What's going on?" Rosemary asked more calmly.

"I'm not sure. Someone tried to take care of the FBI, as near as I could tell."

Tymons groaned.

"It wasn't us," Rosemary snapped at him. "Jesus, Leonard, use your head."

"We should abort," was the answer. "We don't have any more control. We have no choice, we have to abort." He twisted around to look at the major. "Joseph, the FBI isn't going away now, you know that. No more just having a look around and running back to D.C. They're going to dig. And they're going to find something."

Tonero gripped Rosemary's leg briefly to keep her silent. "Leonard, I want you to pay attention."

"Joseph, we—"

"These people," and he indicated the MPs, "are looking for a shooter, okay? Not us and ours. There is no connection, and no connections can be made. Use your head, Doctor, use your head."

Tymons jumped as if slapped. "I don't know. They're going to ask questions."

"Well, that's no problem," Rosemary answered. "We'll just make sure there isn't anyone around to answer."

Tonero looked at her in astonishment.

She shrugged. "We may not have complete control, but we still have some." Her smile was cold. "Simple suggestions ought to do it."

"Jesus!" Tymons shoved his door open. "You're crazy, Rosemary. And as Project Director, I forbid it." He slammed the door and stalked away.

Tonero didn't look, didn't care where he was going. What he cared about was this new woman beside him. Something had changed since a few hours ago. Something drastic. He wasn't sure, but he thought he liked it.

"You better leave," he said quietly.

"And the problem?"

He gave her his best smile. "In for a penny, Rosie. In for a penny." He patted her knee. "Use your best judgment. Just be sure, all right? Whatever you do, just be sure." Then he grunted and took her arm to stop her. Ahead, he saw a man and woman helping a second, somewhat disheveled man out of the woods. *Shit*, he thought.

"Rosie, I think you'd better stick around a minute."

"You are not dead, Mulder," Scully complained. "Don't lean so hard."

She couldn't help a smile, though, at his melodramatic sigh. He might be different, but he was still a man, not above playing sick and injured to the hilt.

Someone called to them, and they stopped on the road.

"Well," Mulder whispered. "Well, well."

A man in uniform fairly marched toward them, and, when he was close enough, quietly demanded a report on Mulder's condition. When Scully balked, he ducked his head in apology. "Sorry. Major Joseph Tonero, Agent Scully. Air Force Special Projects." His smile turned to Mulder. "This incident happened on my watch, so to speak, and I apologize for being slow getting here. A late lunch with an old friend. But I don't have to tell you how concerned I am. Is everyone all right?" Before she could answer, he rubbed his hands together. "Good, good. I'd hate to think what would happen if we lost an FBI."

His smile was intended to be warm, but Scully didn't buy it. The man was less a career soldier than a politician, she decided as she briefed him; his medical knowledge doesn't go much farther than using a bandage.

As soon as she was finished, two others came up behind him—a tall, balding civilian, and too nervous for her peace of mind, and a striking, hard-edged blonde whose bearing was military, but she too was civilian. Neither spoke much save for a perfunctory mumbling of sympathies.

The major introduced them as part of his team, offering their services should the need arise. Scully assured him matters were well in hand, but thanked the officer for his concern.

"As a matter of fact," she added, "we were going to see you this afternoon, when we were done."

Mulder opened his mouth, closed it when she stepped in front of him and put a heel down on his foot to keep him silent.

"Corporal Ulman worked for you, isn't that right?"

The major grew solemn. "Yes, he did, Agent Scully. A tragic loss. He was a good man. And I've been working closely with the Provost—"

"He was going to marry your sister," Mulder said over her shoulder.

Tonero didn't miss a beat: "There was talk, yes. But just between you and me, I don't think it was going to happen." He sighed. "However, I certainly owe it to her to assist you in any way possible."

Neither made any mention of the phone call to Senator Carmen.

"Who attacked you?" Dr. Elkhart asked suddenly, sharply.

"There were two," Mulder answered before Scully could stop him.

"Really?" the major said, grabbing his hat against a gust. "I had no idea."

Scully was relieved when Mulder didn't elaborate; she watched instead as Dr. Tymons whispered something to Elkhart and hurried back down the road, one hand massaging the back of his neck.

"Major," she said, "I'm not sure, it's too soon, but if Agent Mulder here needs more assistance than I can—"

"Walson is mostly shut down," the major interrupted stiffly. "We function primarily as an outpatient clinic now, with only a few long-term patients. Cutbacks." He shrugged a *you know how it is* before the smile returned as he clapped his hands once. "However, the important thing is that you're all right, Agent Mulder." He turned to Scully. "He is all right, isn't he?"

She nodded. "But he could use some rest now, Major, so if you and Dr. Elkhart don't mind, I'd like to get him back to his room."

The major nodded, shook hands all around, and ushered Elkhart away, pausing only to have a brief animated conversation with the MP captain in charge of the search.

"What do you think?" Mulder asked when they were alone.

"I think," she said without turning around, "that there's a shooting incident, and the major brings scientists along instead of doctors."

She checked the car they'd ridden out in, the shattered glass and punctures, at the one shredded, flat tire.

"Hank," she said quietly, "get us a ride to the motel."

Then she looked at Mulder, and instantly knew what he was thinking:

you're not protected, Mr. Mulder, you're still not protected.

THIRTEEN

It took a while before Webber was finally able to get them back to the Royal Baron. Once there, as a doctor, not a partner, Scully ordered Mulder to bed with an ice pack and aspirin until she returned from a visit with Sam Junis. He didn't protest. Just a crooked smile and a phony sigh, and she knew he wouldn't sleep; he'd be too busy trying to squeeze the obvious so it ended up looking like a goblin.

Licia she found in their room, transcribing her notes from the Radnor interview. "Shorthand," the agent said apologetically. "Can't keep up otherwise, and I hate recorders." As she slipped the papers into a briefcase, Scully asked her what, if anything, she'd found out.

"It was like she didn't care," Licia complained, the insult to justice clear in her tone. "And even though she has exercise stuff—says she uses it when she remembers—in that downstairs room off the office, she still drinks like a fish." Then she smiled. "She knew the corporal, though."

"How?"

The smile became a smug grin. "It seems the engaged to the major's sister corporal enjoyed an occasional R&R. Like, nearly every weekend."

"Did she say who he was with?"

"No name, and she only got a glimpse. The corporal, it seems, was very careful. I don't know if that has anything to do with anything, though."

Scully agreed before hustling Andrews into her coat and outside. Webber would watch Mulder in case the shooter tried again, or Mulder decided to have an adventure on his own.

They took the second car, and on the way, she filled Andrews in, ignoring the comments and the outrage.

It also helped her think.

It was evident they were dealing with two different suspects. Aside from the fact that Mulder had been attacked by someone other than the shooter, she was certain the murderer of Ulman and Pierce hadn't suddenly decided to switch to a rifle as his weapon of choice. He was too good with the knife. And a knife was more personal, requiring close range; a rifle was too remote, dispassionate, requiring little or no victim contact at all.

When she had proposed this on the way back, both Mulder and Webber had agreed, but neither could find a reasonable explanation of why, suddenly, they were faced with two opponents.

"Maybe somebody's protecting the goblin," Andrews suggested.

"It's not a goblin," Scully snapped. "Please, don't you start, too. Mulder's already got Hank thinking that way."

"So what do I do? Call him Bill?"

"I don't care. Just don't call him a goblin!"

Andrews laughed and shook her head. "Boy," she said, "he really gets on your nerves, doesn't he?"

Scully didn't answer.

The doctor's bungalow was in only marginally better condition than those of his neighbors, its saving grace a large front garden whose arrangement and vivid blossoms signaled a great deal of time taken and care bestowed. The doctor himself was on the tiny front porch, sitting on the railing, smoking a cigarette. He seemed to be in his early fifties, his greying hair plastered straight back from his forehead; and despite the wind and the chill, he was in shirtsleeves and jeans. Most of him was lean, but his arms were hugely muscled, all out of proportion to the rest of him.

"Popeye," Andrews muttered as they took the narrow slate walk toward him.

Scully almost laughed aloud. She was right; all the man needed was a corncob pipe and a sailor's cap to complete the image.

"Been having a time of it, haven't you," he said by way of greeting. Then he nodded to a police scanner on a small table behind him. "It's either that or Oprah." He grinned.

Scully liked him immediately, and wasted no time getting into his reports. He took no offense at her questions, and asked no questions about the way Andrews barely took her gaze from the surrounding woodland.

The interview didn't last long—Junis agreed with her reconstruction of Pierce's murder, and actually apologized for not getting better photos. He also suggested that the knife used wasn't ordinary. "Sharp as hell, sure," he said, "but the cut of it, I think it might have been heavier than you'd find in your average kitchen."

"Like what?" Scully asked.

"I don't know. I've been thinking about it, but I still don't know."

She knew then she had to ask the next question, and for once, she was glad Mulder wasn't with her. "You had some notes in the margin."

He laughed as he flicked his cigarette onto the lawn. "Yeah. Goblin, right?"

"What does that have to do with anything? As far as your examinations went, I mean."

"Not much." He pulled another cigarette from his pocket and stuck it between his lips. He didn't light it. "Nothing. I'd just been to see Elly Lang, had to calm her down a little with a mild sedative, and that's all she talked about." A sideways glance. "You heard about it, huh?"

"We talked to her, yes."

Junis followed the wake of a pickup heading west. "Don't think she's crazy, Agent Scully. Don't write her off. I don't know who she saw, but she's no fool."

"She was drunk, Dr. Junis."

He laughed abruptly, loudly, until his eyes began to water and his face reddened alarmingly. "Sorry." He laughed again and wiped his eyes with a sleeve. "God, I'm sorry." He gripped the railing with both hands. "Drunk? Elly? You've been listening to Todd Hawks. Nope, never. She goes to that bar for the company, that's all. She's outlived her family, has no real friends to speak of. She has one drink, a Bloody Mary, that she nurses until she's ready to go home, and that's about it. That woman has never been drunk a day in her life."

"Then what about the spray paint?"

Junis watched another truck pass. "Because she believes it, Agent Scully. She believes it as sure as you believe there ain't no such thing. That doesn't mean she's certifiable."

Scully wasn't so sure about that, but she didn't know enough to pursue it. Instead she asked about the other witness.

"Fran?" Junis lowered his gaze to the garden. "I can take you to her, if you want, but she won't do you a whole lot of good."

"Why not?"

His expression hardened. "The heroin she took that night was damn close to an overdose. I brought her to a facility up near Princeton." He paused. "A mental rehab, by the way, we don't have anything like that around here. She was pretty far gone." He lit another cigarette and blew smoke into the wind. "She'll recover from the overdose most likely, but as for the other . . . she isn't going to be released for a long, long time."

Swell, she thought; just what I need—an addict who probably can't even recognize her own reflection. Interviewing Fran Kuyser quickly dropped toward the bottom of her list.

"Do you sit out here a lot?" Andrews asked then, not bothering to look at him.

He nodded to Dana, not at all fazed by the sudden change of subject. "Guess I do, come to think of it. I like to watch the world drive by, see who's going where. People around here, those that work on post or at McGuire, they have their military doctors, and the others . . ." He shrugged. "Not a lot left, but I guess you already noticed that."

Scully also noticed that he didn't seem to mind. Although he was too young to step down yet, he appeared to be resigned that this practice wasn't going to get him a retirement home in a better location, and that, for whatever reason, was all right with him.

"Oh, we have our moments," he said, startling her. "And it beats all to hell working an ER."

She wasn't inclined to disagree, thanked him for his time, and told him where she was staying in case he thought of something else.

"I already know that," he said. And grinned.

Back in the car, Andrews shook her head in disbelief. "You know, you can't breathe around here without somebody knowing it. Hardly any privacy at all." She forced herself to shudder. "That's too weird for me."

Dana grunted, but she wasn't really listening. There was something not quite right here, something she and the others had missed. She didn't think it was tied directly to the killings, but it was, somehow, important. Small, but important. She knew Mulder felt it as well. In spite of the afternoon's attack, she knew it bothered him, and maybe by the time they returned to the hotel and he had rested, he would know what it was.

As long, she added glumly, as he doesn't call it a damn goblin.

The motel lights were all on when they returned, highlighting the crown facade, flooding the parking lot with dull silver, making the clouds seem even lower and thicker than they were. After sending Andrews to fetch her interview notes, she pushed through Mulder's door just in time to hear him say, ". . . a multitude of sins."

"What sins?" she demanded. "And why aren't you in bed?"

He sat in shirtsleeves at the room's tiny table, his back to the wall, papers spread in front of him. Webber was on the bed, propped up by pillows, knees drawn up to serve as a rest for a legal pad.

"Hi, Scully," Mulder said. "I'm cured."

Webber refused to meet the rebuke in her eyes as she dropped into the chair across the table. "You're not cured, and you've been working." But the scolding was, as always, a waste of time; he would only give her one of two looks— the hurt little boy, or the sly-fox, lopsided grin— and do what he wanted anyway.

He settled for the grin. "We've been checking up on Major Tonero."

"It's weird," Webber commented from the bed. "His office confirms he's head of Air Force Special Projects, like he told us, but they wouldn't explain what that means."

"Which," Mulder continued, "covers a multitude of sins." He shook his head slowly. "Curiouser and curiouser. Why would an Air Force major, who isn't even medical personnel, be assigned to an Air Force hospital on an Army post? Which, for the most part, is used as training for reservists, and a jumping-off point when troops have to get overseas in a hurry." Then he pointed at her before she could answer. "And don't tell me there's a perfectly rational explanation."

Oh, Lord, she thought; he's in one of his moods.

"And," Webber added eagerly, "why would he be so interested in the ambush? And why were his people there, too? Those two doctors, scientists, whatever."

Scully stared at him for so long, he began to look embarrassed. "Well . . . it's a good question, isn't it?" He scratched the back of his head. "I mean, isn't it?"

"Yes, Hank, it is," Mulder said when Scully didn't answer. "And I'll bet I have a possible answer."

"Mulder," Scully said, her voice low and warning. "Do not read into this more than there is."

"Oh, I'm not," he protested lightly. "I'm not even going to begin to suggest that maybe these goblins have something to do with the major." He leaned back in his chair. "I wouldn't think of it."

"Of course you wouldn't," she said. "Because you already have. Now look, we've got a—"

Andrews walked in then, smiled a not very sincere apology for being late, took a reluctant seat on the bed, and said, "So now what?"

Dana checked her watch; it was after five. "So now I think we'd better break for a while and have something to eat." A look shut Mulder up. "There's been too damn much excitement around here, and I want us to cool down for a while before we end up on horses."

"What?" Hank said.

"A definition of confusion," Mulder explained, hands clasped behind his head. "He jumped up on his horse and rode off in all directions." He winked. "Scully likes wise sayings like that. She hordes fortune cookies, you know."

Hank laughed; Andrews only snorted and shook her head.

Dana, for her part, did her best not to react, because she recognized the signs—he was high on an idea, the bits and pieces of the puzzle beginning to give him some kind of picture. The problem with him was, that picture was often one no one else saw but him.

It was what made working with him at once so fascinating and so damn exasperating.

Rather than try to derail him, however, it was better to give him his head and go along for the ride. For a while.

So she suggested they clean up and meet in the restaurant in half an hour or so for coffee. Her tone brooked no argument. When Andrews left without a word, Scully's expression sent Hank along as well, deciding it would be a good thing to take a walk around the building.

When they were alone, Mulder's expression sobered. "I saw it, Scully. I'm not kidding, I really saw it."

"Mulder, don't start."

He spread his hands on the table. "It's not like I'm the only one, you know. Even Chief Hawks admitted there were others." He held up a palm to keep her quiet. "I saw it—okay, just a glimpse—but I also touched it. It wasn't my imagination, it wasn't wishful thinking. I touched it, Scully. It was real."

She leaned away from him, thinking. Then: "I'll grant you it was real. He was real. But it wasn't any goblin, no supernatural creature."

"The skin—"

"Camouflage. Come on, Mulder, Fort Dix is a training base. That means there are personnel who are experts in all sorts of weaponry . . . and camouflage. God knows how elaborate they can be, but it's probably a lot more now than just smearing greasepaint on your face."

He tried to stand, grimaced, and sagged back. "My jacket."

It had been tossed on the dresser. She fetched it and looked it over.

"I hit it twice, once pretty hard." He leaned forward under the light. "There's nothing there, Scully. No paint, no oil, no nothing."

She dropped the jacket onto the bed. "A suit, that's all. Skin-tight, latex, who knows? No goblins, Mulder. Just people in disguise." She pointed at the bed. "Lie down."

She knew he still wasn't feeling well when he made no cracks, just nodded wearily and shifted stiffly to the mattress. As he settled down, she brought him a glass of water and aspirin and watched him drink.

"What about the major and his people?" he asked. His eyelids fluttered. "Hank's right, that's kind of fishy."

"Later," she ordered. "You're not doing anybody any good, least of all yourself, when you can't think straight." Her frown deepened. "Get some rest. I'm not kidding. I'll drop by later to see how you're doing."

"What about the others?"

She smiled prettily and headed for the door. "Oh, I think we'll manage. We'll muddle through somehow."

She opened the door and looked over her shoulder. He hadn't closed his eyes; he was staring at the ceiling.

Then his gaze shifted. "Scully, what if I'm right?"

"Rest."

"What if I'm right? What if they're out there?"

She stepped out, the door closing behind her. "They're not, Mulder. For God's sake, rest, before I—"

"How do you know they're not? You can't see them, Scully. They're out there, somewhere, and you can't see them."

FOURTEEN

The room was empty.

X Rosemary didn't really expect to find anyone there; it was too soon after the woodland incident, and it also wasn't easy for it to get away without being noticed.

What she hadn't expected, however, and what frightened her, was the destruction.

She stood on the threshold, one hand absently rubbing her arm, a faint chill slipping across the back of her back. Although she couldn't hear it, she swore she could feel the wind pummeling the hospital, could feel the building's weight settling on her shoulders.

The notion made her angry, but she couldn't shake it off.

Damn, she thought, and passed a weary hand over her eyes.

The mattress had been sliced open in a score of places, the stuffing strewn across the floor; the desk was overturned, one leg snapped off; the chair was little more than splinters.

The Blue Boy had been yanked off the wall and shredded.

In its place, scrawled in black letters:
I'm looking for you.

Major Tonero sat at his desk, hands folded on the blotter, staring at the telephone.

He was neither panicked nor overconfident, but since leaving the site of the shooting, he had begun to review his options. By the time he had stopped pacing the office, he knew what had to be done. And it galled him. Not that he considered the Project a failure; too much had been learned from it, too much progress gained. No, what galled him was—

The telephone rang.

He listened to it without moving.

At the seventh ring he cleared his throat and picked up the receiver.

"Good afternoon, sir," was followed without prompting by a detailed summary of what had happened that afternoon, and what connection he suspected it had with the two incidents he had previously reported to those in charge. He spoke crisply and flatly, no emotion at all. When he finished, he listened.

He did not interrupt, speaking only when asked a question, his spine rigid, his free hand still flat on the blotter.

The voice at the other end was calm, a good sign, but he did not, could not, put himself at ease.

When the conversation arrived at the crux, thirty minutes had passed.

The last question was asked.

Tonero nodded. "Yes, sir, I do, with your permission." He inhaled slowly. "I believe it's time to explore other venues; there are several mentioned in my December report. This one, through no fault of ours, has been contaminated. I also believe the additional personnel now on site will not be put off, most especially after this afternoon's incident. That they are from the Bureau means we can neither control nor contain them with any true degree of effectiveness or guarantee of success. However, I have no doubt we can make the transfer without discovery, and then the Bureau people can investigate all they want. They won't find a thing."

He listened again, and for the first time, he smiled.

"Yes, sir, I do believe you're right—sometimes you win, sometimes you lose. But we are still light years ahead of where we were the last time. This, I think, argues well for our eventual success."

His smile broadened.

"Thank you, sir, I appreciate that."

The smile vanished.

"Indispensable? No, sir, to be honest, he is not. His objectivity and full commitment have been lost, I believe, and, frankly, his nerves are shot. I do not believe another relocation would be in the Project's best interest. Dr. Elkhart, however, has been most helpful. It would be a severe loss if she were not to remain."

He waited.

He listened.

"Forty-eight hours, sir."

He nodded.

He replaced the receiver and for several long seconds sat without moving.

Then, as if he'd been struck across the shoulders, he sagged, and whispered, "Jesus!"

His hands began to tremble, and there was sweat on his brow.

Barelli sat at a window table in the diner, beginning to wonder if he had, in fact, wasted his time. Not that he didn't doubt his reporter's skills; that he was good was a given. But after nearly an hour with that police sergeant, with some comments from the others as they drifted in and out of the station, he had learned practically nothing he hadn't known before—Frankie was dead, the killer was still out there, and nobody had a clue what the hell was going on.

And that goblin shit—Jesus Christ, what the hell did they think he was?

A round-faced wall clock over the register ticked closer to six as he sipped at cold coffee and stared at the traffic. The weather hadn't discouraged anyone, it seemed. Men in uniform, soldiers in civilian clothes trying not to look like soldiers, strolled or drove past, filling the diner, moving into the bars that served food, lingering in front of the movie theater a block west of the police station.

Friday night in the middle of nowhere.

His stomach complained of all the caffeine he had drunk, and he popped an antacid tablet into his mouth, chewed it absently, and wondered what the hell he was going to do now. Of course, there was still that "date" with Babs Radnor to keep. If he wanted to. And right about now, it looked as if it was the only game in town.

Another antacid, another scan of the street, and he dropped a few bills onto the table and went outside.

He scowled at the overcast. He hated this kind of day. If it was going to rain, he wished it would do it and be done with it; otherwise, why the hell didn't those clouds just blow away?

He headed for the corner; his car was still parked in front of the police station.

Along the way he passed an old woman dressed in black from a heavy topcoat to a long scarf wrapped around her head. She held a large purse close to her chest, and an idle glance there made him stop and turn slowly.

What he had seen was the orange top of a

spray paint can, and it didn't take a genius to figure out who she was.

He hurried after her, came abreast and said, "Miss Lang?"

She stopped and glared up at him. "*Ms.* Lang, if you don't mind. Who are you?"

"I'm a reporter," he explained, best smile, best voice. "I'm looking into the . . ." He lowered his voice, slipping her into his confidence. "Into the goblin affair."

He waited patiently, watching her debate both the truth and the sincerity of what he had said.

A bus coughed past them.

Three young airmen on the corner broke into song.

Elly Lang eyed him suspiciously. "You think I'm a nut?"

"He killed a friend of mine. That's not crazy at all." When she didn't walk away, he touched her arm lightly. "I'd be pleased if you'd join me for dinner."

"And pump me, right?" she snapped.

The smile turned up a notch. "That, and for the company."

She shook her head. "You're full of it, mister, but I'm not going to pass up a free meal." She took his arm and led him up the street. "You going to be cheap, or are we going someplace good?"

He didn't laugh, but he wanted to; instead, he promised her the best meal this town could provide, which seemed, for the moment, to satisfy her. And as long as he didn't run into Mulder or

Scully, he had a feeling this was going to be a most informative, and lucrative, night.

Tonero wasn't in his office, wasn't anywhere on post that she could tell, but Rosemary ordered herself not to panic. There was still time to make corrections. There was still time to salvage something of the years she had put in.

She returned to the hospital, nodding silently to the receptionist and making her way down a corridor to an elevator stenciled AUTHORIZED PERSONNEL ONLY. From her pocket she took a small key ring and inserted a silver key into a vertical slot where, ordinarily, a summons button would be. When the door slid aside, she checked the hall and stepped in.

The key took her down.

She didn't bother to watch the floor indicator; the elevator only stopped at three levels—the second floor, where the major's office was, the main floor, and a subbasement.

The car stuttered to a halt and the door opened; she stared uneasily down the length of the dimly lighted corridor.

It seemed a lot longer tonight, and her heels a lot louder on the concrete floor.

The faint thrum of distant machinery was the only other sound.

As if performing for an invisible audience, she made a show of smoothing her smock over her chest, of caressing a palm over her hair as she walked. Confidence, outside and in, was the key. As long as she kept to her plan, as long as she didn't lose her head, everything would be fine.

She tested Tymons's office door; it was locked.

She opened the Project Center door and nearly screamed when she saw him bending over one of the computers.

"Jesus, Leonard," she said, stepping in. "I didn't know you'd be here. What are you—"

He turned to face her, and in his right hand was a rectangular block of black metal about six inches long. In his left hand was a gun. "Just stay where you are, Rosemary, all right? Just . . . stay where you are."

"Leonard, what the hell are you doing?"

He smiled wanly. "Correcting a few things, that's all."

She looked around the room, not seeing anything out of place until her gaze reached the first computer screen. Though the machine was on, the screen was blank. So was the second one.

He waved his right hand. "It was so easy, I don't know why I didn't think of it before." He held up the block. "Why go through the whole mess when all you need is a magnet."

"My God, Leonard!"

"One pass, and poof!" He dropped the magnet on the shelf. "Poof. All gone."

Outrage prevented her from speaking, and fear of what Joseph would do when he found out.

"The thing is," Tymons said calmly, and put a bullet through the nearest computer.

She jumped, but the gun kept her from fleeing.

"The thing is, you see, nobody's ever really going to know, are they? I mean, there's no sense going to the papers or the TV stations, because no one would ever believe it."

He shot another one, showering the floor with splintered plastic and shards of glass.

She took a step back.

He glanced at her sideways, his expression rueful. "I'm still going to try, though. Despite the odds, I'm really going to try."

"You can't," she said hoarsely, her throat lined with sand. She cleared it and tried again. "You can't." Her left hand fluttered helplessly from her chest to her throat and back again. "All those years, Leonard, all the work we've done. All the time. For God's sake, think of all the time!"

"All the failures," he said flatly. "All that time, and all those failures." He spat dryly. "Buried, Rosemary. We had to bury our failures."

He's insane, she thought; my God, he's insane.

"Listen, Leonard, if that's what . . . if you don't care about the work . . . think about—" She jerked a thumb at the ceiling. "You can't."

"Why? You mean those stupid oaths we signed?" He fired at the third and last monitor and hunched a shoulder to protect himself against flying shards. "Meaningless, Rosemary. By the time I'm through, they won't mean a thing."

"I'll deny it," she threatened. "I'll tell anyone you tell that I don't know a thing."

He straightened. "My dear doctor, I'm sorry, but you won't live long enough to have the chance."

She backed up hastily until the wall stopped her, the open door to her right. She couldn't think, could barely breathe, and a small fire in the workings of one of the destroyed computers had begun to lift feathers of smoke into the room.

"They'll come after you, Leonard," she warned, swallowing hard, fighting the nausea that roiled in her stomach. "Even if you can get off post, you won't be able to hide for long. A week, maybe a month." Sweat stung her eyes, but she didn't dare move her hands to wipe it away. "You've just signed your own death warrant."

He shrugged. "Like I care, Rosemary? Like I really give a damn?"

Without warning he emptied his clip into the shelves, the explosions deafening, damage almost total. She couldn't help but scream then, more in rage than fear, hands up to protect her face from the spinning, flaming debris. Before she could move, he had replaced the clip with a fresh one from his pocket.

And pointed the gun at her head.

Her eyes fluttered closed.

All she could think was *This is crazy, this is wrong*.

"Go away."

She didn't move, didn't understand.

"Rosemary, go away."

When she looked, the gun was at his side, but the defeat in his voice wasn't reflected in his face.

"Maybe," he said, "you'll last longer than I."

Disgust twisted her features, but she refused to say a word for fear he would change his mind. Although she wanted desperately to rail against the destruction of all their work, she wanted more desperately to get out of this alive.

"Go away," he whispered, and shook the gun at her.

Without further urging, she bolted clumsily into the corridor, and hadn't taken two steps toward the elevator when she kicked herself in the ankle and fell hard into the wall. She cried out, more in surprise than pain, and cried out again when she heard a gunshot.

Another.

At that she ran, keeping her stinging arm braced against her side, fumbling with her free hand for the keys.

At the elevator door the key slid off the control plate twice before she was able to insert it properly. "Come on, damnit," she whispered urgently, willing her nerves to settle down. "Come on, come on!"

The door opened and she virtually threw herself into the car, spun around and inserted the key a second time.

It wasn't until the door had hissed closed that she realized she wasn't alone.

No, she thought; not after all this, no.

"You know," said a rasping voice behind her, "I'm getting pretty good at this, don't you think?"

FIFTEEN

X Andrews wasn't in the room when Dana returned, and she decided to take some of her own advice and scrub some of the afternoon away. Maybe some time alone would help her figure out the purpose of today's attack.

So little of it made any real sense.

If it had been meant as intimidation, as a warning to stay away and drop the investigation—for whatever reason—it certainly wouldn't work, and surely whoever was behind it knew that as well; if it had been meant to stop them permanently, that had failed, too, and she couldn't convince herself that the shooter hadn't been aiming to kill.

"Unless," she thought aloud, "he wasn't an expert."

She pushed a hand back through her hair, and rubbed the back of her neck. There had been a lot of wind, lots of leaves and things blowing around. Branches moving, targets moving. Plus, they had been shooting back.

So maybe, she thought, just maybe, they had gotten a little lucky.

That particular idea unnerved her more than anything. Especially when she realized that the shooter really could have killed her and Webber at practically any time before they had ducked into the trees.

They had been in the open far longer than Mulder.

But he hadn't.

The more she thought about it, the more she believed he had only been trying, and succeeding, to pin them down. To take them out of the game as much as he could.

What he had actually been trying to do was put a bullet in Mulder.

The man at the Jefferson Memorial:

you have no protection, Mr. Mulder, you still have no protection.

"Oh, brother," she whispered. "Oh, brother."

Think. She needed a clear head to think this through, or she'd end up just as paranoid as her partner.

Once stripped and in the shower, however, it wasn't the shooter she concentrated on—for some reason, she couldn't stop thinking about Mulder's other assailant. The explanations she had given him were more than likely correct, or at the very least, parameters. Which did not, under any circumstances, include anything like a goblin.

And yet . . .

She made a noise much like a growl.

And yet there had been times past when she had been forced to the unwelcome conclusion that explanations could very well be only rationalizations in disguise.

She growled again and turned away from the shower head, letting the hot water slam against her back and splash over her shoulders. Her eyes half-closed. Her breathing steadied as she willed the memory of gunfire to a safer distance.

Steam rose gently around her, condensing on the narrow pebble-glass window in the white-tiled wall, running down the translucent sliding door.

She felt nothing but the water.

She heard nothing but the water.

The perfect time, she thought suddenly, for good old Norman Bates to slip into the bathroom, knife held high and at the ready. Effectively deaf and vision blurred, lulled by the comfort of steam and heat, she wouldn't know it was over until the end had begun; she wouldn't know, because all she could see was a smeared shadow on the door.

Standing there.

Watching.

Biding its time.

The shadow, of course, was the drape of bath towels over their rack by the door.

She knew that.

No; she assumed that.

Her eyes closed briefly as she damned Mulder for sparking her imagination; nevertheless, she couldn't stop herself from holding her breath to brace herself, and opening the shower door, just a little.

Just to be sure.

"Mulder, I swear I'm going to strangle you," she whispered in relief and mild anger when she saw the towels, and the rack, and not a single place in the tiny room for anyone to hide.

The steam flowed over and around her, twisting in slow spectral ribbons, creating the momentary illusion she had stepped into a light fog.

She shivered.

The room was chilly.

And the steam that should have filled it flowed and twisted, because the bathroom door was open.

He didn't want to sleep.

There was too much to do.

But the pain had finally ebbed, weariness taking its place, and he couldn't keep his thoughts in an orderly line. They drifted, fading and dancing.

mulder, watch your back.

Patches of skin like snapshots, flashing too

rapidly for him to focus on, barklike skin without the roughness of bark, without the texture, although he couldn't really be sure because contact had been so brief.

mulder

The voice was muffled by sleep and time, yet it sounded maddeningly familiar despite the fact that it belonged to no one he knew; a roughness here, too, and forced, as if the speaker, the goblin, was either suffering low-level pain or hadn't yet gotten used to the voice that it had.

watch your back.

And if it was true, that he had to watch his back, why hadn't he been killed, like the others?

I don't know, he answered, but the voice and the nightmare wouldn't stop.

Rosemary couldn't take it anymore. Her knees buckled, and she sagged weakly to the floor, her back against the elevator wall.

"Are you all right?"

Hoarse, painful to listen to.

She nodded.

"What happened?"

Gone, all gone, she thought; everything's gone and Joseph will kill me and it's gone, damnit, all gone.

"Dr. Elkhart, what's wrong?"

She raised her head and gestured defeat.

"Dr. Elkhart, say something. You're scaring me."

"My dear," she said with a brittle bitter laugh, "you have no idea what scared is."

A shuffling, a shifting, a soft hand brushing across her ankle.

"Can I help?"

She made to shake her head, and stopped. She stared at the elevator door, seeing the two of them, reflections twisted out of recognition in the polished steel, and before long she felt her lips pull back into what might have been a smile.

"Yes," she said at last. "Yes, dear, I think you can."

Scully's purse was on the floor between the toilet and the tub. She reached through the gap and fumbled it open, pulled out her gun, and straightened, staring intently at the bathroom door, still open about an inch. Her left hand shut the water off; her right wrist slid the shower door away.

Once on the bath mat, she grabbed a towel and wrapped it hastily around her; it was no protection at all, but it made her feel less vulnerable. Her teeth chattered and her lower lip quivered as the room's chill raised a pattern of gooseflesh on her skin.

She switched off the light.

Water dripped too loudly from the shower head.

The only illumination in the outer room came

from the brass lamp on the nightstand between the two beds, just as she had left it.

There was no sound or movement.

Using her left hand, she opened the door as slowly as she could, crouching low until she could slip over the threshold and duck behind the nearest bed. The gun barrel swept the room just ahead of her, but no one else was there.

Don't assume, she told herself; never assume.

Feeling like a jerk now—*never assume, Scully, never assume*—she half-crawled around the footboard to be sure her visitor wasn't hiding between the beds. Once satisfied she was indeed alone, she sat on the mattress and tried to remember if, maybe, she hadn't left the bathroom door open by mistake; or maybe she had closed it, but the latch didn't catch; or maybe Andrews had returned, heard the shower, and decided Scully didn't need to be disturbed.

But if that were true, if she had heard the shower, why had she opened the door?

A trickle of water slipped out of her hair and down her spine.

"All right," she said aloud, as much for the sound as the comfort. "All right. It's all right, you're alone."

That didn't stop her from turning on the hanging lamp over the table to help banish the room's shadows, or from drying off as fast as she could, with the bathroom door wide open. Once that was accomplished, dressing was quick and easy—blouse, skirt, matching wine jacket. By then she was almost calm, and she looked in the dresser mirror as she smoothed the blouse over her chest, deciding that one of these days, Bureau or not, she would get herself a fashion life.

Back into the bathroom, then, to wield a brush through her hair, using her reflection as a sounding board as she practiced telling Mulder what his stupid notions were doing to her. It didn't help. Her reflection just gave her the same sardonic look he would when he heard. If he heard. By the time she was finished, she had decided this was something her partner did not need to know.

A lopsided smile sent her into the front room, where she started and gasped when she spotted someone pacing her at the corner of her vision.

"Listen carefully," Rosemary said urgently. She stabbed a thumb at the door. "He's trying to destroy us. Tymons. He's afraid, and he's a coward. He doesn't care about you, me, or the Project. He wants . . . he wants us all dead."

A silence then, and she held her breath, praying.

"He didn't approve of me from the beginning, you know." Still hoarse, now with sullen rage. "He thought I was too . . . emotional."

Rosemary agreed silently.

A giggle: "He's really scared of me, you know."

"Yes. I know."

The giggling stopped. "What can I do? I'm not stupid, Dr. Elkhart. I know what'll happen if you stop helping me. What can I do?"

Rosemary tried to think, tried to set the priorities that would keep her intact.

"Do you need him? Dr. Tymons?"

There wasn't a second's hesitation: "No. No, we don't."

"Others?"

"Three," she said without having to think. Then concern made her stand when a wrenching cough made her wonder if they could pull it off. "Can you do it, dear? Are you well enough?"

"I can do it. Really. But it'll take time. A couple of days, maybe. I can't—"

The coughing increased, grinding into spasms that made Rosemary reach out a hand, grip a shoulder, and squeeze until it was over.

"It's okay," she whispered, rubbing now, soothing. "It's going to be okay."

And she believed it. It would be all right. Everything would be all right.

Then she spoke the names.

Scully's right hand was already reaching for the gun on the bed when she realized the movement was only her reflection in the dresser mirror.

Too damn many mirrors around here, she

thought sourly, and pointed at it as if to order it to find someone else to scare.

She froze.

Something moved on the wall behind her. A slight movement she would have missed had she simply glanced in that direction.

She watched, waiting, thinking maybe it had only been a shadow cast by a passing car.

It moved again, and she turned and made her way between the beds.

A moth fluttered its wings slowly and began to make its way toward the ceiling.

Fascinated, licking her lips, she climbed onto the bed, balanced herself, and looked away.

Looked back, and it took a full second before she could find it again.

"Well," she whispered.

A tentative smile came and went.

Then she bounced on the mattress, just high enough to snatch the moth away in a loose fist. Feeling its wings beat against her palm. Whispering to it as she opened the door and flung it away. Standing back, rubbing her chin thoughtfully.

She needed another test, and footsteps outside made her think fast.

With the hanging lamp on again, the nightstand lamp off, she sat on the far bed and pushed herself back until she rested against the headboard, legs crossed at the ankles. She could barely see herself then, but she could see just the same.

A key turned in the lock.

She heard it but didn't move.

The door opened and Licia stepped in. "Scully?"

Dana opened her mouth, but kept silent.

Andrews headed for the bathroom. "Scully, you in there? Look, are you going to leave me with that boy all night? Damn, you should hear—" She pushed the door open and cut herself off, sighed, turned, and yelped when she noticed Scully sitting on the bed, pointing at her.

"Jesus!" Her hand splayed across her chest. "God Almighty, Scully, I didn't see you there. Why the hell didn't you say something?"

Scully smiled. "You didn't see me."

Andrews scowled. "Of course not. It was dark. You're sitting in the dark."

Scully pushed at the hanging lamp. "Not really. But you see me now, right?"

Andrews didn't know how to answer, her lips working without a sound. Finally she said, "Well . . . yes. I guess so." She laughed at herself. "Of course I do. The light was—"

Scully pushed off the bed, shoved her gun into her purse, and reached for her coat. "Go get Hank," she said. "Meet me at Mulder's."

"Again?"

"Again." Scully pushed her gently but firmly outside. "God help me, but I have a feeling Mulder is right."

Andrews gaped. "Goblins? About the goblins?"

"Something like that." She couldn't believe she had just said it. "Yes, something like that."

SIXTEEN

Wrapped in nothing but a thin stubby towel, Mulder examined his reflection in the steam-shrouded mirror. He looked drawn, and probably a little too pale. But he certainly didn't look like a man who had almost been killed. Twice in the same afternoon. However a man like that is supposed to look, that is. He rose up on his toes and inhaled sharply when he saw the full extent of the size and shape of the bruise below his ribs. That, he knew, was going to be hell in the morning.

He toweled off slowly so as not to aggravate either the bruise or the hammer and anvil gearing up in his skull. Deliberately slowly, because, as Scully had already sensed, he had begun to feel

that electric spark of anticipation, the one that signaled the true beginning of the hunt.

He suspected that right now, Webber was
having fits, and Andrews was pacing whether she
was standing up or not. It was only natural. A little ordinary poking around had ended up in a
deadly firefight, and they probably couldn't stop
the adrenaline from flowing. Action, they no
doubt thought, was the key now, not methodical
investigation. It didn't matter that nothing but
casings had been found at the site, and nothing at
all at the site of his ambush.

Action. Get moving. Keep moving. Sitting
down, having coffee, talking things out, was definitely not the way things were supposed to be.

As he dressed, he glanced around the room,
not really seeing the furniture or the dingy walls.
Hints and whispers had come to him while he'd
let the warm water and steam do their work.

Hints and whispers.

Not all of them clear.

Still, the fever dreams he had had—and there
was no other way to describe them—refused to let
him go. Every throb in his skull, every touch of fire
below his ribs, reminded him of what he had seen.

Not what he thought he had seen.

He slipped stiffly into his jacket, stuffed his
tie into one pocket, and grabbed his topcoat.

And stopped.

What he should do now was head straight for
the Queen's Inn to meet the others.

Or he could slip away for a while, away from Scully's watchful doctor's eye, and—

The door opened suddenly.

He stumbled back, tripped over the edge of his bed, and fell on the mattress, his head nearly exploding.

"Jesus," he said angrily.

Scully looked down at him without any sympathy at all. "I have an idea," was all she said.

Major Tonero sat on the porch of his modest Cape Cod on the outskirts of Marville, a cigarette in one hand, a tumbler of scotch and soda in the other. Although he had been expecting the FBI to call on him since meeting those agents this afternoon, he wasn't disappointed when they hadn't. Their attention was elsewhere now. Whoever had ambushed them had unwittingly done him a great favor.

Now all he had to do was tell Rosemary about his conversation with their superiors, and they could begin the relocation procedure. By Sunday afternoon they would, with a little luck, be on their way.

He sipped, and blew a smoke ring.

It was chilly tonight, but not enough to keep him inside.

Besides, he preferred it out here. The neighborhood was small, quiet, so perfectly ordinary that there were times, both night and day, when he felt as if his superiors had dropped him into the middle of a television series, circa 1955. But it was definitely better than living with *them*, short-sighted and single-minded officers who lived and died for the service without once ever under-standing what true potential there was.

He toasted that truth with another drink.

There were, now that he thought about it, only two problems remaining: what to do with Leonard Tymons, and what do with the Project's subject.

He wasn't worried, though. The answer would come. It always did.

A car sped up the block. He frowned, hating the disruption of his quiet evening, the frown deepening when the car squealed to a halt at the curb. He leaned forward—Rosemary?

After several seconds she climbed out and ran–staggered toward the house. He was up and at the steps before she reached them, taking her arms and hushing her until they were inside.

"Leonard," she gasped, and dropped heavily onto the couch.

She looked like hell; in fact, she looked like a corpse, her hair damp with perspiration, her cheeks flushed with an unnatural color that unpleasantly accentuated her already pale face.

Shit, he thought angrily; why the hell can't it be easy, just for once?

"Tell me," he said, keeping his voice low.

He didn't move when she told him what had

happened at the Project lab, didn't touch her when she began to tremble so violently she had to hug herself to calm down, didn't offer a word when she finished and looked up at him, beseeching him for comfort.

He turned to the window and looked out at the lawn, hands clasped behind his back.

When he turned back, he smiled. "Are you sure he's dead?"

"He . . . he has to be by now."

"There were backups, correct?"

She passed a hand over her face, forcing herself to think. "Yes." She nodded hesitantly. "Yes, of course. Although I don't know how recent they would be. Leonard was always—"

"No matter." He took a step toward the couch. "In his office?"

"Yes."

He rubbed the side of his nose thoughtfully. "And what about our friend?" His eyes widened in slight alarm and he glanced at the front door.

"No, don't worry." She inhaled deeply, slowly, and leaned her head back wearily, closed her eyes, as her left hand unbuttoned her coat and pulled it away as if she needed room to breathe. "We were in the elevator, and then . . . I don't know where."

Another step: "I'm correct in assuming that, without the proper medication, our friend will eventually . . ." His smile flashed and vanished. "Fade away?"

"Damnit, Joseph, what's the matter with you? Haven't you listened to a word I've said?"

He held out his hands, palms up, beckoning until she took them and allowed herself to be pulled to her feet and into his arms. He kissed her ear, her cheek, her lips.

"Joseph?"

She was cold; cold with fear.

And trembling.

He whispered of the telephone call, and of the problems he had had until the problems, it seemed, had decided to take care of themselves. He whispered of the support he had given her to those in charge during that call. He suggested, in a whisper, that they take her car back to the hospital, to Dr. Tymons's office, and retrieve the backup computer disks. Although no one had access to the Project level except themselves, it seemed as if they might be leaving earlier than expected.

"Or," he whispered after she snuggled, wriggled closer, and kissed him back, hard, "we could always wait until morning."

It was her turn to whisper as she began working on his shirt: "Joseph, you can be one arrogant bastard, do you know that?"

"But for good reason, Dr. Elkhart. And don't you ever forget it."

Barelli almost felt guilty leaving the old woman alone at the Company G, but since everyone there seemed to know her, and like her, the guilt passed as soon as he was outside.

It had been, from the beginning, an evening of surprises.

The establishment itself, around the corner and halfway down the block from Barney's, was a low clapboard building outlined in soft blue neon. In its large front window a neon trooper marched guard duty around stencil-style letters that spelled out COMPANY G. A shiny black film over the glass prevented anyone from seeing inside, but once through the door he had been pleasantly surprised. The restaurant–lounge was a single large room, softly and indirectly lighted, with black plastic and glass, gleaming chrome and brass. A bar ran along the left-hand wall, and the carpeted floor held a score or more tables, about half of which were taken. A dance floor took up most of the back, with a low stage against the wall.

The food, too, had been more than decent, and the drinks inexpensive. Elly Lang ordered well and ate carefully, as if expecting to make the meal last all night. When he asked her about herself, she smiled and told him little except for the reputation the community had given her.

All because of the goblins.

By the time he had finished he knew he had heard all she had to say. Not ranting, exactly, but it sounded like a story she had told a hundred times, and not much different from what he had learned at the police station.

She had, pleasantly, dismissed him when his mind began to wander, and although he stopped short of kissing her on the cheek, the almost-gesture had made her laugh and shoo him away.

Now, on the street, he considered returning to the station to have a talk with the dispatcher. Because of their job, they usually knew more than anyone, and he remembered Sergeant Nilssen telling him their regular operator was a young woman, Maddy Vincent.

Which was when he remembered his date with Babs Radnor.

"Shit," he muttered. "Damn."

He would have to go back and make some kind of excuse. She had been taken with his reporting reputation, he knew that much, so maybe she wouldn't be all that unhappy when he assured her he wasn't about to head home right away. A rain check until tomorrow seemed the most likely way out.

He hurried up toward Main Street, changing his mind about driving, deciding that a phone call would do. If he played it right, sounded right, she might even be excited for him, now and later.

He shivered then and wished he had brought a topcoat with him.

True night had settled over the town, starless, feeling like rain. Houses and buildings slipped into the protection of the dark, neon and street-lamps giving the street needed color, and a semblance of life it didn't have when the sun shone.

There were just enough pedestrians to make the district seem almost lively; a street cop spoke to a disgruntled knot of teens; a cruiser trolled slowly westward, not caring about the traffic it backed up behind it; several shops were open late, ghosts of customers inside.

The wind had died.

Still, he hunched his shoulders as he hurried westward, grumbling when he reached the police station without finding a public phone. He looked over, shrugged a *what the hell*, and took advantage of the first break to sprint to the other side. Once in, he had to wait for several minutes. Unlike his earlier visit, tonight the station was busy—two cops leading two lurching drunks back toward the cells, the radio in constant chatter, a man in plainclothes at a desk arguing with two women, one of whom had a bloody bandage wrapped around her hand. When he finally caught the desk sergeant's attention, he was told brusquely that Officer Vincent wasn't on this shift, he would have to wait until morning.

He couldn't.

The idea had taken hold, and now he couldn't shake it.

A handful of smiling lies inflating Vincent's importance to his story gave him an address and directions; a flourish of notebook and pen proved to the officer that Barelli wasn't about to spell his name incorrectly.

By the time he was back on the sidewalk, he realized he was out of breath.

Easy, boy, he thought; take it easy, don't blow it now.

Two blocks up, one block down, the sergeant had told him. An easy walk, and a chance for him to think of the questions he'd need to ask.

The house was easy to find—it was the only one on the street without any lights.

He knocked, rang the bell, even wandered around to the back door and knocked again, but Officer Vincent wasn't answering.

No matter, he decided, and parked himself on her front steps; she has to come home sometimes, and when she does, I'll be waiting right here to make her famous.

He sat, he smoked, he listened to the neighbors on the left have a beast of a battle. He walked around for a while to keep warm, but always within sight of the house. And when he checked his watch under a streetlamp and realized it was only a few minutes past eight, it occurred to him that Maddy Vincent might not be home for hours. It was Friday night, and she was single, and what the hell had he been thinking?

He was nearly at the corner when he stopped cursing his stupidity and trotted back across the street, pulling his notebook out of his jacket pocket. Just to be sure she'd be around, he would leave a note. Not too obvious, a little mysterious. Pique her policewoman's interest. He would save the sweet talk for when he saw her.

It took him four tries before he was satisfied

and tore the page free. The next thing was a place to put it so the wind wouldn't blow it halfway to the next county.

He settled for folding it in half and sticking it between the door and the frame.

Then he turned around, dusting his hands, and saw the shadow standing on the porch.

"Who the hell are you?" he demanded.

"It doesn't make any difference," the shadow said.

Barelli didn't see the blade until it was too late, and there was nothing left to do but open his mouth and try to scream.

SEVENTEEN

X A single light over the table, barely reaching the first bed, and the second one not at all.

Scully sat with her back to the window, Mulder by the door, Webber on the edge of the dresser, Andrews on the edge of the near bed.

Mulder didn't like it. He couldn't see expressions; they were too much like spirits at the fringe of a seance, floating in and out of the dark as if they wore veils.

Scully's fingers pushed at nothing on the table's wood-grain surface. "I've been thinking about a moth I found on my wall."

She hadn't seen it right away, not only because it was too small, but also because its

192

coloration almost blended in with the paint.
That made her think of camouflage, and the
goblin, who was able to hide in an alley without
being seen, and hide in the woods without
Mulder seeing. Despite what she had said
before, she couldn't quite bring herself to
believe that tactics like that were supported by
an arsenal of camouflage suits and greasepaint,
burnt charcoal, twigs and leaves worn as aids to
blending in.

Although it was possible, it also required
advance knowledge of where the target victim
would be.

"And I don't think such a package could be
carried on someone's back. It would be inefficient
and clumsy."

There was, for example, no way the killer—
the goblin, if they had to call it that—could have
known that Grady Pierce would pass by that
alley that night, at just that time. Webber's interview with the bartender had established that
more often than not, Noel brought the ex-
sergeant home himself. And they themselves
hadn't decided to visit the site of Corporal
Ulman's murder until they had finished lunch in
the diner.

"Two questions," she said, eyes down, as if
speaking to the table.

"How did it know where to be?" Webber said.

She nodded.

"Unless it knows magic," Andrews said, a

smile in her voice, "how could it be ready with . . . whatever it wore to hide itself?"

Scully nodded again.

Mulder watched her fingers move, dusting, tracing circles.

"For now, let's set aside the why of it, the killing. And the who." She looked up, too pale in the light, and Mulder looked away. "The how, on the other hand . . ."

No one spoke.

A car backfired in the parking lot, and only Webber jumped.

An engine raced on the county road, another followed, and there were horns.

Mulder shifted stiffly as he watched her face. It bothered him sometimes, how smooth it was, without many lines, because it prevented him from really knowing just what she was thinking. Too often a mask. But her eyes, they were different. He could see them now, shadowed by the light over her head, and he could see that she was struggling with a reluctant decision.

He brushed a strand of hair from his brow.

The movement made her look, and when she looked, she inhaled slowly.

"Special Projects," said Webber, startling them all. "That Major Tonero and his Special Projects."

"I think so," she answered. "But exactly what, I'm not sure."

"Yes, you are," Mulder said gently. "It's not a goblin, at least not like Elly Lang says it is."

Andrews made a faint noise of derision. "So what is it? A ghost?"

"Nope. It's a chameleon."

The wind rose.

A draft slipped through the window and fluttered the curtains.

Andrews slapped her thighs. "A what? A chameleon? You mean, a human chameleon?" She waved a hand in disgust. "No offense, Mulder, really, but you're out of your mind. There's no such thing."

He didn't take offense, although he knew she wanted him to. "There are lots of things that are no such thing, Licia. Some of them aren't, some of them are." He scooted his chair closer to the table. "I think Scully's right. This is one of them that is."

Andrews appealed to Scully. "Do you have any idea what he's talking about?"

A corner of Scully's mouth pulled up. "This time, yes."

He made a sour face at her, then swiped at his hair again. "A chameleon—"

"I don't need a biology lesson," Andrews snapped. "Or zoology. Whatever. I know what they can do."

"They change colors," Webber said anyway. "To fit their background, right?" He stepped away from the dresser. "Wow. Do you really think this is what we've got?"

Mulder held up a finger. "First, you're wrong. Sort of. Chameleons can't change color to fit every background. They're limited to only a few, like black, white, cream, sometimes green." He grinned. "Put him on a tartan tablecloth, he'd probably blow his brains out."

Webber laughed, and Scully smiled.

Mulder's fingers began to tap eagerly on the table. "But within certain limits, yes, he can adjust his pigmentation."

"I don't believe this," Andrews muttered. "I swear to God, I don't believe it."

Mulder ignored her; he wanted Scully to follow and watched her as he spoke, in case he made a mistake.

"Now, contrary to popular opinion, chameleons don't change at will, right?"

She nodded.

"It's things like temperature or emotion that cause the coloration to alter. When they get scared or angry. I don't think they sit down at breakfast and decide to be green for a day." He sat back, then stood.

"Careful, Mulder," Scully cautioned.

"But we can't do that," he said to Webber. "Right?"

"Change color? Hell, no. Except when we get tan or something."

"Right." He moved to the door, snapping his fingers at his side, turned and gripped the back of his chair. "But suppose our Major Tonero and his group—Tymons, right? and Elkhart—suppose they've been able—"

Around the edges of the drapes he spotted flashing lights and yanked open the door. In the parking lot below he saw a police cruiser, warning bar alit and swirling color. A patrolman looked up. "Hey, you the FBI?" he called.

Mulder winced and nodded.

The policeman beckoned sharply. "The chief wants you right away. We got another one."

Two patrol cars, parked sideways, and a quartet of orange-stained sawhorses bracketed a fifty-yard section of the street. An ambulance was parked nose-in to the curb, and two attendants leaned against it, smoking and waiting. Blue and red lights swarmed across branches and tree trunks, and the faces of two dozen onlookers gathered on the sidewalk opposite the scene. Flashlights danced in back yards, and in the distance a siren screamed.

There was very little talk.

Mulder and Scully followed their driver around the barrier; Webber and Andrews were behind them in the other car.

Hawks met them at the foot of a gravel driveway. "Man walking his dog," he said, pointing to a young man standing in the street, a terrier in his arms. "He found him." He sounded angry.

"Are you sure it's the same?" Scully asked.

Up the drive two men knelt beside a body in high grass between the gravel and the porch; one of them was Dr. Junis.

"See for yourself."

Mulder moved first, but he didn't have to go all the way before he saw the victim's face. "Damn!" He turned to block Scully. "It's Carl."

"You know him?" Hawks demanded.

Scully inhaled sharply and stepped around the two men, nodding as Junis glanced up and recognized her.

"He's a reporter," Mulder explained, disgust and sadness in his voice. "A sports reporter."

"Sports? Sports, for God's sake? So what the hell was he doing here?"

"Corporal Ulman's fiancée was his cousin. He wanted me to come up and look around. I guess . . . I guess he was doing a little looking on his own."

"Jesus." Hawks clamped his hands on his hips, glowering, breathing heavily. "Son of a bitch, what the hell's going on around here? Mulder—" He stopped and wiped a hand over his face. "Mulder, is there some shit you're not telling me?"

A man on the porch called the chief, who hesitated before telling Mulder to stay where he was. When he left, Mulder scanned the growing crowd, and the shadows the cruiser lights created between the trees, between the houses. It was bad enough when the victim was a stranger, but this . . . He crammed his hands into his pockets and stared at the ground until footsteps on the gravel made him look up.

"Come on," Scully said gently, her voice trembling slightly.

Hawks called them from the steps, and held out a piece of paper found jammed into the door-frame. It was a note from Barelli, requesting an interview which, he promised, would be paid for by a complete dinner at the best restaurant in town.

"Who lives here?" Mulder asked.

The house was rented by Maddy Vincent. The day-shift dispatcher, Hawks added. A gesture to figures moving around the inside told him the woman wasn't home, and no one knew where she was. "No surprise, it's Friday night," the chief said in disgust. "Shit, she could be in Philadelphia for all I know. Or . . ."

Mulder checked the porch, the blood on the flooring and on the door. Carl was attacked here, he thought, and the force of the attack, and his probable retreat from it, sent him over the railing. Where he bled to death without ever getting his story.

"Damnit," he said, and stomped down the steps. "Damnit!"

An hour later, Carl's body was gone and those neighbors who'd been home had all been interviewed.

No one had seen anything; no one had heard

anything. A call had gone out to Officer Vincent's friends in the vain hope she hadn't left town. A check with the station told them Barelli had stopped in only a short while ago, specifically looking for the dispatcher.

"But why?" Hawks leaned heavily against his patrol car, his face drawn and tired, his voice hoarse. Most of the crowd had retreated to nearby houses; two of the cruisers had left. "What the hell did he think he knew?"

Mulder held up a small notebook. "Nothing that he wrote down." He handed it over. "He had dinner with Miss . . . Ms. Lang, and wanted to see your dispatcher. All he had were more questions."

"He's not the only one," the chief growled.

Mulder sympathized with the man's frustration, but it didn't extend to telling him about the major. That, he decided grimly, was someone he wanted to talk to himself, without the complications Hawks was bound to create.

The chief finally mumbled something about getting back to his office, and Mulder wandered over toward his car, where the others waited. They said nothing as he turned to stare at the empty house, ribboned now in yellow, a patrolman on the steps to keep the curious away. The dusting had been completed, but he doubted they would find any useful prints besides Barelli's and Vincent's.

Goblins, he thought, don't leave handy clues.

He was angry. At Carl, for playing in a game

well out of his league, and at himself, for the helplessness he felt for not knowing enough. It was a waste of energy, he knew that, but there were times, like now, when he simply couldn't help it.

He walked back to the middle of the street and stared at the house, ignoring the damp wind that whipped hair into his eyes.

Carl was a big man, and definitely not soft. He had to have been surprised. A single blow, and it was over. He had to have been surprised.

"Mulder." Scully came up beside him. "We can't do any more here."

"I know." He frowned. "Damn, I know." He rubbed his forehead wearily. "Major Tonero."

Scully looked at him sternly. "In the morning. You're exhausted, you're not thinking straight, and you need rest. He's not going anywhere. We'll talk to him in the morning."

Any inclination to argue vanished when she nudged him into the car; any inclination to do some work on his own vanished as soon as he saw the bed.

But he couldn't sleep.

While Webber snored gently, and murmured once in a while, all he could do was stare at the ceiling, wondering.

Finally he got up, pulled on his trousers and shirt, and went out onto the balcony, leaning on the railing while he watched the trees across the road move slowly in the slow wind.

He thought of Carl and the times they had had; he thought of the man who had tried to kill him that afternoon, an afternoon that seemed years distant, in another lifetime; he shivered a little and rubbed his arms for warmth as he wondered why Carl had wanted to talk to Officer Vincent. Elly Lang was obvious, but what did Hawks's dispatcher have to do with the goblins?

"You're supposed to be sleeping."

He didn't jump, didn't turn his head. "The day you figure out how to turn off my brain, Scully, let me know." He shook his head, but carefully. "Amazing, isn't it."

"Your brain?" She leaned her forearms on the railing. "It's okay, but I wouldn't call it amazing."

"Chameleons," he said. He nodded toward the woods. "Somewhere out there somebody has figured out a way, maybe, to create natural protective coloration in a human being. I don't know what you'd call it. Fluid pigmentation?"

"I don't know. I'm not sure that's—"

"It was your idea."

"Yeah, but I still don't know. Do you have any idea what kind of genetic manipulation that would require? What kind of control on the cellular level that would mean?"

"Nope." He glanced at her sideways. "But if you tell me, maybe I'll be able to get some sleep after all."

She rolled her eyes as she straightened. "Go to bed, Mulder. Just go to bed."

He smiled at her back, suddenly yawned, and did as he was ordered.

Sleep, however, was still hard to come by.

Aside from the aches in his head and side, he couldn't help thinking about the possibility that there could be someone in the room right now, standing against the wall there.

Invisible, and watching him.

Waiting.

And he wouldn't know it until a knife tore out his throat.

EIGHTEEN

There was no dawn.

There was only a gradual shift from dark to shades of grey, and a falling mist just heavy enough to keep windshield wipers working, to raise the sharp smell of oil and tar from the black-top.

Mulder was not in a good mood.

Following Scully's orders, Webber had let him oversleep, and it was close to ten before he finally opened his eyes to a note on the pillow that told him the others would be waiting in the Queen's Inn.

He was also not miraculously cured. Although his head seemed fine except for a small lump beneath his hair, his side felt as if it had been set in

204

cement. Every time he moved, he thought his skin would rip open.

He supposed he ought to be grateful for the extra healing time, and for the concern Scully showed him, but knowing that didn't make it happen. He showered and dressed as quickly as he was able, thinking that he would eat quickly, check with Chief Hawks on the slim to none chance there had been any new developments overnight, and then . . . he smiled mirthlessly as his brush fought with his hair . . . then he would have a few words with Major Joseph Tonero.

His stomach growled as he knotted his tie, and he snarled at it to hold its horses. Then he grabbed his coat, stepped outside, and was pleased to see that the weather perfectly complemented the way he felt.

I live for days like this, he thought gloomily as he descended the center staircase.

Scully recognized his mood immediately, and after a quick check to be sure he was all right, she hustled them through breakfast and outside, with a reminder that while they were heading for the post, there was also someone else out there, the shooter, they had best not forget.

Andrews still thought the so-called goblins and the shooting were related; when no one rose to the bait, she slumped into her corner and glared at the passing scenery.

There was no sound then but the rhythmic thump of the wipers and the hiss of the tires.

It wasn't until they had passed through town that Mulder remembered wanting to have a word with Hawks. He punched his leg lightly and scowled, and ordered himself to get with it, or he'd blow it all because he wasn't thinking straight.

Once this is done, he promised; I'll talk to him when we're done here.

Fifteen minutes later they passed between two simple brick pillars that marked the post entrance. No guards, no guardhouse; a stretch of woods that quickly fell away to the post's main complex—barracks, administration buildings, and on-post housing. A transport plane from McGuire lumbered and thundered overhead. A squad of troopers double-timed across an intersection, their dark green ponchos slick with water. They passed a construction site for a new federal prison twice before Scully finally gave up and made Hank ask directions. An MP gave them, and within minutes they were on New Jersey Avenue; it didn't take them long to find what they were after.

"Brother," Webber muttered as he pulled up in front of Walson Air Force Hospital.

It was a seven-story light tan brick structure, but it somehow seemed a lot smaller.

Because, Mulder realized, it was mostly empty. A lot of empty rooms and offices, a lot of space for things to happen without anyone being any the wiser.

He sat up and watched the entrance, something quickening inside when he noted that hardly anyone went in, and no one came out.

"What makes you think he'll be here?" Andrews asked, rousing herself from her sulking.

"If he's working on a project," Scully answered, "he will. Something like this doesn't often hold over weekends."

Something like this, Mulder thought.

"But do we have any authority?"

Mulder opened the door, slid out, and poked his head back in. "We've been asked in by a U.S. senator, Licia. The senator the major himself called. So if he wants to argue, he can write his congressman."

A civilian receptionist sat just inside the entrance, a multiline telephone and a logbook the only items on her small desk. Mulder wished her a good morning, showed her his ID and asked directions to Major Tonero's office. She wasn't sure the major was in, and because of her standing orders was reluctant to give him the instructions until he insisted; then she pointed to a bank of elevators to their left.

As they moved away, he heard a noise and looked back.

Webber had his finger on the telephone's cutoff button. "I don't think so," he said politely, with a wink. "Government business, okay?"

Mulder couldn't believe it when the woman suddenly grinned. "Sure. Why not?"

Pancakes and women, he thought; the guy's got it made.

The major was in.

But it didn't look to Mulder as if he'd be there very long.

The office was a two-room suite on the second floor. When Mulder ushered the others in ahead of him, he saw a handful of packed cartons against one wall, and an empty bookcase behind what he assumed was Tonero's secretary's desk. The door to the inner office was open, and he gestured the others silent as he approached it. He could see the major standing in the middle of the room, back to the door, speaking quietly but angrily to someone seated at his desk.

"Damnit, Rosie, I don't give a damn who—" He turned and saw Mulder, and forced a smile. "My goodness, Agent Mulder, what is this, a raid?" He laughed as he shook Mulder's hand and nodded to the others.

The person behind the desk was Dr. Elkhart.

Mindful of protocol and egos, Mulder allowed Tonero to direct the conversation, politely answering questions about his health while he noticed that Dr. Elkhart, in a lab coat, was not as composed as she wanted him to think. Although she sat back in the major's chair, her legs crossed, her hands on the armrests, her cheeks were lightly flushed, and her attempt at a bland expression was nearly a total failure.

She was, he thought, royally pissed off.

What, he wondered next, is wrong with this picture?

"It's a real tragedy about Carl," Tonero said, stepping back to perch on the edge of his desk, ignoring Elkhart completely. "I want you to know that I am not going to rest until this matter is solved."

"I appreciate that, Major," Mulder said, sensing rather that seeing Scully take a chair just behind and to his left, while Webber and Andrews flanked the door. It was a large room, but their positions and attitude now made it seem much smaller. "I can assure you that we're not going to let it rest either."

He smiled quickly.

Dr. Elkhart uncrossed her legs.

"Well, good!" Tonero smiled purposefully at each of them in turn before rubbing his hands briskly together. "And what can I do to help?"

Mulder raised his eyebrows—*Gee, sir, I'm not really sure*—and glanced at Scully as if looking for guidance before facing the major again. "Well, I guess you could tell me what your project has to do with goblins."

Tonero sputtered into a laugh that proved he could appreciate a good joke when he heard one; but the laugh faded into a scowl when neither

Mulder nor the others joined him. His back straightened; his expression became somber.

"I'm sorry, Agent Mulder, but what we do here is classified. I'm sure you understand."

"I do, believe me," he answered agreeably. "The DoD can be pretty tough sometimes."

"Absolutely. Now—" He waved one hand to indicate the closing and packing he had to do. "As you can see, we're being transferred—the orders came just this morning—and we're in a hell of a mess." A look over his shoulder that Dr. Elkhart ignored. "Dr. Tymons—you may recall meeting him yesterday—seems to have gone ahead without telling us, so it's kind of hectic around here at the moment."

He stepped forward, with the intention of easing the agents back into the outer room.

Mulder sidestepped around him, his right hand brushing across the edge of the desk before he leaned on it and turned his head. "Dr. Elkhart, where were you last night? I don't know, about nine?"

Elkhart started, and blinked. "What?"

"Last night," he repeated.

"Now look here, Agent Mulder," Tonero snapped. "Dr. Elkhart is one of our most—"

"Home," the woman answered, crossing her legs again. "I was home. Watching TV." Her smile was crooked. "Why, Agent Mulder? Am I a suspect?"

Mulder matched the smile, didn't answer the

question as he turned his back to her. "And you, Major?"

"How—" Tonero's face darkened. "What do you think you're doing? Do you know who—"

"Chameleons," said Scully mildly from her chair.

"Lizards," Elkhart responded immediately, not quite as mildly. "Not, I'm afraid, from the goblin family."

"Goblins?" The major's voice rose. "Goblins? What are you talking about? What does some old woman's rantings have to do with my cousin's murder?"

Mulder shrugged. "I don't know, Major. But just as you have to explore all possibilities within the scope of your projects, so do we, in murder investigations." He turned to Scully. "Do you think we should come back later? I think they're in a hurry."

Scully agreed and headed for the door with the others.

Mulder, however, didn't move. "Major, can I assume you'll be around later this afternoon? Just in case?" He scanned the room. "Looks like you have a lot of work left here. And in your project office, too, I would guess."

"Absolutely, absolutely." Tonero moved again, and this time Mulder gave way. "Just call ahead, if you don't mind. I have—" He gave Mulder a brief martyred look. "Superiors, if you know what I mean. This relocation makes them nervous."

"I'll bet," Mulder said. "Nice to talk to you again, Dr. Elkhart," and was gone before the woman could reply.

Once in the silent corridor, the door closed firmly behind them, he held up a palm to keep the others from talking, then checked left, toward the elevator bank, before looking in the opposite direction, where he saw another, single elevator. A snap of his fingers sent Webber there on the silent run, and a sign that told him there was no button to push.

"Well?" Andrews demanded when they reached the lobby.

"Well," Mulder said, "they sure don't make majors like they used to." He took his left hand out of his pocket and held out his palm, showing them the key ring he'd lifted from the major's desk.

"Not a word, Scully," he said lightly when she began to object. He told Webber and Andrews to get back to town and track down Aaron Noel, Barney's bartender, to see if the man knew how close Pierce and Ulman had been, and if Barelli had been in asking questions.

"And find out where that dispatcher—"

"Vincent," Webber said.

"Right. Find out where she was last night, what time she came home. You know the drill."

"What about you?"

Mulder shrugged. "If we leave now, whatever this key takes us to will be gone before we get back. We're going to snoop around a little."

"But isn't that against—"

Mulder hushed him with a look and hurried outside with them.

The post looked deserted.

Nothing moved but a light rain that shifted now and then as a light wind passed through it.

He opened the door for Andrews, then stood back and wondered what the mighty Douglas would say when he found out that the other car was Swiss cheese and useless. He could see Webber and Licia arguing heatedly inside, but with the windows up, he couldn't hear a word.

He almost intervened, rolled his eyes and changed his mind. That woman will be the death of me yet, he thought, and wished they'd be gone. Now. He wanted to be sure; he didn't want them suddenly turning up again.

The car jerked forward a few feet and stalled.

He smiled gamely and decided to get inside before he added pneumonia to his ills. He mimed giving the car a push with one foot, waved when Webber saw him in the rearview mirror, and trotted back to the lobby when the engine fired and held. The receptionist was clearly puzzled, but he assured her they had only forgotten something in Major Tonero's office and would be gone before she knew it.

The woman seemed to doubt it.

"Mulder," Scully said as they walked purposefully toward the elevator bank, "if we get caught . . ."

He didn't answer.

After a check over his shoulder, he took her elbow and ducked around the corner.

The corridor was empty, and only half the lights embedded in the ceiling's acoustic tiles were lit.

Whispers from the front, echoing softly.

He found the right key on the second try, and held his breath until the door opened onto an empty car. Once in, he inserted the key again and sent them down.

Scully said nothing; she had been on this road with him too many times before. The obligatory warning had been given—if we're caught; now she would be focused.

He wouldn't disturb that; it was too valuable.

He only hoped the major was still too angry to think straight, and realize what was going on.

NINETEEN

The corridor was short, and the air not quite stale. No ceiling lights here—just a hooded bulb at the far end, and one at the entrance. The floor, like the walls, was unpainted concrete.

"Like a bunker," Scully whispered.

In and out was the order of the day. They hurried to the first door, and Mulder turned the knob. It was unlocked and, when he looked in, empty. A desk, metal shelves on the wall, a small, open safe on the floor beside the desk, and a blackboard.

Nevertheless, they searched, checking drawers and corners. Tonero had said that Tymons was already gone, but Mulder doubted it was to the relocation point. By the looks of it—the papers and pads left behind in the desk, the handful of books on the shelves—this room had been emptied in a hurry.

"I smell gunpowder," Scully said, returning to the corridor. "And smoke." She wrinkled her nose. "Something else. I'm not sure."

The middle door was unlocked as well, and open a few inches. Mulder pushed it with his foot and stood back, shaking his head.

"Jesus."

What was once on the single shelf was now on the floor, smashed and scattered, some of it scorched or charred. He counted the hulks of at least three monitors and a pair of keyboards; he counted at least a half-dozen bullet holes in the wall beneath what looked to be a one-way window.

Without speaking, they sifted through the wreckage, not knowing exactly what they were looking for, knowing only that they'd know when they saw it. Then Scully rocked back on her heels.

"Mulder."

He joined her, dusting his hands on his coat, and saw the blood. Lots of it, dry, and buried beneath plastic and blank sheets of paper.

"Not a gunshot wound, I think," she said.

"Goblin."

"I don't know. It's been here a while, though." She poked at a large stain with a forefinger. "But not that long. We're not talking about days."

He guessed that the room on the right had

been Tymons's office, and Tymons's alone. It didn't have the feel of being shared with someone, like Rosemary Elkhart. This one had been the Project's heart and control center. From here . . . he stood at the shelf and looked into the next room.

"Oh, boy," he said. "Scully."

She looked, and her eyes widened.

Mulder checked his watch. "Time, Scully. Not much left."

The last room was a shambles as well, but it was the walls that fascinated him—one cream, one sand, one green, one black.

His fingers began to snap unconsciously.

This was it.

This was where the goblin was tested. One wall, one color.

Scully wasn't sure. "So what did they do, Mulder? Line him up against the wall and wait? They could have done that with a sheet on a bed."

Mulder looked at her sharply, and looked around the room again. His lips moved as if he were talking to himself before they parted in a satisfied grin. "Training," he decided, and stood against the cream wall, unable to disguise the excitement in his voice. "Scully, it's a training room." He pointed. "Bed, desk, CD case there in the corner. Somebody lived here—no, somebody stayed here temporarily, maybe overnight, maybe for several days at a time." He spread his arms along the wall. "Somebody who—"

Scully whirled on him. "Don't say it, Mulder! I'm having a hard enough time as it is. Do not make it more complicated than it has to be."

"But it's not, Scully," he insisted, pacing now, rubbing at his chin, his cheeks, pushing a hand back through his hair. "This is where the goblin learned how to change." He turned in a slow circle. "Learned how to *will* the change, Scully, not wait for the change to happen." He took a step toward her, and was stopped by her frown. "You said it yourself, right? He can't carry every contingency around on his back. It's impossible. Even for the most basic circumstances, it would be, for him, a dangerous hindrance."

He looked to the door.

"A trained killer needs as few obstacles as possible. He needs a smooth way in, a smooth way out. No stops along the way for adjustments to a costume. No ripples. The quicker, the better."

He looked around again, closer now, searching for something, anything personal, that would give him a hint to the room's sometime occupant. But there was nothing left, and there was nothing left of the time he had hoped they would have.

On the way back to the elevator, Scully ducked into the control room and came out folding several pieces of paper she tucked into her shoulder bag. Blood samples. Not, Mulder thought, that they really needed them.

He knew who the blood belonged to.

• • • •

On the way through the lobby, Mulder dropped the keys onto the absent receptionist's desk, then followed Scully outside, anxious to get back to town.

The light rain had grown heavier, the air darker for it.

Another squad of soldiers marched by, absolutely silent.

"Mulder," Scully said, "in case you haven't noticed, we don't have a ride."

It hadn't occurred to him, and he didn't think it mattered.

"And we don't have an umbrella, either."

She slapped him lightly on the arm and returned inside to use the phone.

He didn't follow.

He watched the rain.

A human chameleon, he thought, slipping his hands into his pockets. An effective assassin, who could theoretically slip through the tightest of cordons.

In, and out.

No ripples.

Or, more frighteningly, a small army of them, living shadows slipping through the night.

No ripples.

Only death left behind.

It wasn't a perfect disguise. It probably wasn't effective in broad daylight, and the goblin—he couldn't stop thinking of it that way—

wouldn't be able to stay in the same room for very long. Even Scully had eventually spotted the moth.

Nevertheless . . . living shadows.

He shifted from foot to foot impatiently.

No question about it, Major Tonero was the project's shepherd. He knew all of it, which meant he probably knew that Tymons was dead. Killed by the goblin? If so, was the goblin under the man's direction?

But why kill the head of such a project?

Too easy—Rosemary Elkhart was second-in-command. There was no reason to believe she couldn't, or wouldn't, take over if she had to. And the best way to ensure that would be to make herself indispensable to those who were in charge. He pictured her in the major's chair, and suddenly realized that was what had bothered him earlier. *She* was in *his* chair. She was comfortable using it. She had used it before.

"Well," he whispered. "Well, well."

"Stop thinking, Mulder, and move it," Scully told him. She snapped open a large black umbrella, took his arm, and hustled down to the sidewalk.

They hadn't gone a dozen paces before he took it from her before she poked his eye out. "Where did you get this?"

"You'd be surprised what you'll find in the ladies' room on a rainy day." She hugged his arm tightly, quickly. "I called Chief Hawks, he's on his way to pick us up."

"So why—"

"The major isn't going to stay in that office, Mulder, not when he finds out his keys are gone. He'll check that setup first, using Dr. Elkhart's keys, then probably come after us. I would like to be long gone before that, if you don't mind."

"He'll follow us."

"No, I don't think so. We can't disappear, Mulder. The senator, remember?"

He almost stopped then, but her momentum pulled him along.

"Carl."

"What about him?"

Mulder stared into the rain, willing Hawks to come in at speed. "According to his notes, he was asking around about the goblin." His chest tightened, his stride quickened. "Cleaning up, Scully. I think someone's scared, and the goblin's cleaning up."

The telephone rang only once before Rosemary snatched up the receiver. She listened and said, "What are you doing, calling here? Suppose *he* had answered?" Without thinking, she began to weave the cord between her fingers. "Well, you're lucky he's not. He's downstairs now. Those FBI agents were here, and he thinks they lifted his damn keys." She watched the door without seeing it. "I think, if they didn't know before, they know now."

Her gaze shifted to the window, to the trails

of water almost invisible against the grey air, the grey sky.

She stiffened.

"You can't do that. No. It's bad enough, but you can't touch them."

The goblin cleared its throat painfully. "Yes, I can."

Rosemary almost rose out of the chair. "Damnit, will you listen to me? Just . . . just what we agreed, all right? Don't make it worse than it already is."

"Doctor, I can do whatever I want."

She couldn't believe it. First Tymons, now this.

"In fact, I think all that stuff you've been telling me is plain bullshit."

"Look—"

"You know, I don't think I'm affected much at all." It laughed softly, and wheezed. "And if I am, Doctor . . . whose fault is that?"

She did stand then, angrily shaking her hand until the cord fell off. "Goddamnit, listen to me, you idiot! If I have to—"

"Doctor." The voice was calm. Very calm.

Rosemary closed her eyes and took a deep breath. "What?"

"We have an agreement. I'll do what you want."

She leaned forward, bracing herself on the desk with one hand. "Thank you. It'll be fine, just fine, as long as we don't panic."

"I'll do what you want."

She nodded. "Yes."

"Are you listening?"

"Yes, of course."

"Then don't, Doctor. Don't *ever* talk to me like that again."

"Oh, really? And what if . . . hello? Damnit, hello?"

The line was dead.

She gaped at the receiver, then slammed it back onto its cradle. Calm again; she had to regain calm again, be the eye in the storm. It was not, yet, a disaster that those damn agents probably knew something. They could snoop around all they wanted, but they didn't know it all. As long as she made sure she, and Joseph, didn't panic, they never would.

At least not until it was too late.

But she was afraid for the goblin. Despite her assurances, she knew what little control she had was practically gone. Like all the others, those too deep in the woods to be found—here, and elsewhere—the strain and the treatment had proved too much.

This one had lasted the longest, however.

This one was the proof of her triumph.

She grabbed her purse and coat and hurried from the office. Joseph would have to come to her for a change, once he stopped blowing off pompous steam. She still had some last-minute packing to do.

Just a few more weeks, she prayed as she made for the elevators; just get me out of here in one piece, give me a couple more weeks, and it'll be over.

Really over.

The door slid open as the overhead bell chimed softly.

She took a step, and froze.

The car was empty. She could see that, but she still couldn't bring herself to go in.

With a low groan of frustration she used the fire stairs instead, yanking on her coat, cursing her own weakness, but oddly grateful for the harsh sound of her heels on the steps.

TWENTY

Scully decided her vacation hadn't been nearly long enough, not by half.

A Marville patrol car had picked them up minutes after they left the hospital, just about the time the rain had stopped. The driver, though polite, refused to answer any of Mulder's questions.

"Talk to the chief," was all he would say.

It sounded to her as if Hawks's equanimity at having the FBI in town was being sorely tested.

Now they sped toward town, and she couldn't help feeling that everything was moving too fast. She needed time to think, and she wasn't getting it. She was reacting, rather than acting; otherwise, she never would have taken Mulder's leap from experimental camouflage to full-blown, controlled human chameleon, with no stops along the way.

It wasn't like her; not at all.

She braced herself when the car momentarily lost traction on its way around a bend, and wished she had tried to get a hold of Webber instead. And when the driver said, "Sorry, ma'am" once he regained control, she almost snapped his head off.

Not like her at all.

Then Mulder folded his arms on the back of the seat and rested his chin on them. He said nothing, but she could feel him at her shoulder. Her eyes closed briefly at a flurry of leaves across the windshield.

"Mulder, I'm sorry about Carl."

He grunted.

She realized then that that was part of her problem. She hadn't liked Barelli; he was crude, too slick, and too full of himself. But for reasons she would never understand, he had also been Mulder's friend, and she hadn't said a single word of sympathy, of commiseration. The moment she had seen the reporter's body, she had clicked into professional mode.

She hadn't let the murder touch her.

It had obviously touched her friend.

"We have to get to Elly," he said at last.

She agreed, and asked the driver to take them there instead of the station.

"I don't know," he said doubtfully. "I was told—"

"Don't worry about it," Mulder said. "We'll take the heat. You can tell him we pulled rank. FBI, pushy feds, stuff like that."

For a second, Scully thought the man would flat out refuse. Then he grinned, shrugged, and: "Whatever you say, sir."

"So punch it."

"You got it."

And it took all of Scully's self-control not to grab the dashboard.

Traffic increased as Marville began, Saturday shoppers and wanderers taking their time to make the business district last as long as they could make it. The driver took a back-road, corner-cutting shortcut to avoid the main street, and pulled up smoothly in front of the apartment building.

"You want me to wait?" He sounded hopeful.

"Yes," she told him as she opened the door.

He took the radio mike and called in: "Maddy, this is Spike. We're at the Goblin Lady's place. Maybe the chief should meet us here, huh?"

The radio hissed. "I'll tell him. Watch your back."

"You got it," he said, and hooked the mike back on its cradle.

"That's it?" Mulder asked, sounding disappointed.

"You mean, ten-four, that kind of stuff?" The driver shook his head. "The chief hates radio talk. He says it makes us sound too much like cop shows." He laughed. "Besides, half the guys keep getting the numbers wrong anyway. Maddy knows what we're saying, so . . ." He shrugged.

Scully was already outside, looking up at the bay window. The curtains were closed. She turned slowly as Mulder left the car, and clamped a hand hard against her chest.

"Mulder!"

Immediately she ran across the street without checking for traffic, heading straight for the small park and Elly Lang, sitting motionless on her bench. The old woman faced the empty ball field, bundled in a black coat, a black umbrella canted over her head.

She didn't turn when Scully called her name.

No, she thought, leaping the curb and racing across the wet grass; damnit, no.

"Elly!"

She heard Mulder behind her, drifting to her right to come up on her flank.

"Elly!"

She grabbed the bench back and propelled herself around, damning herself for not thinking of this sooner.

If they were too late, she would personally rip Tonero's medals off, one by one, and pin them back on his bare chest. One by one.

Suddenly a hand snapped out from beneath

the umbrella, and she yelped as she jumped to one side when a stream of bright orange nearly caught her on the chest.

The old woman stared at her without blinking. "Oh. It's you." And she tucked the spray can back into her purse. "I must be getting slow."

Scully didn't know what to say, could only nod while she tried to catch her breath. "I thought—"

"Yes," Elly said. "I can see that." Her gaze shifted when Mulder came up beside her. "They won't hurt me, you know. Never have. I figure they figure an old lady can't do them much harm."

"Ms. Lang," Mulder said, "this one is different."

Scully dropped onto the bench and gently pushed the umbrella to one side. "It's killed at least three people that we know of, Ms. Lang. We think you could be in danger."

Elly humphed. "You don't know much about goblins, young lady." She shook a bony finger in Scully's face. "You should study more. You're a smart girl. You should learn more. Goblins," she said, "don't kill anyone. Never have."

Dana looked to Mulder for support, and he hunkered down in front of the old woman, one hand gently on her knee so he wouldn't topple. "Ms. Lang, this one is sick."

"They don't get sick."

He shook his head. "Not that kind of sick." He tapped his temple. "This kind. It isn't like the others. It's . . ." He swallowed, and let his hand slide away. "It's evil, Ms. Lang. I don't know any other way to put it."

Scully saw it then, the doubt and the birth of fear in the woman's face. Suddenly she seemed two decades older. "You shouldn't be sitting out here," she said quietly. "You should be someplace warm. It'll rain again soon."

"The children," Elly whispered.

"I don't think they'll be playing much today."

She stood, sliding her hand along the woman's coat until she grasped her hand. The fingers twitched, then curled around hers, and she pulled Elly slowly to her feet, the umbrella dropping forgotten to the ground.

Mulder retrieved it as Scully pointed to the cruiser. "See that man there? His name, if you can believe it, is Spike. I think I can talk him into staying with you for a while."

Arm in arm they walked across the grass.

"Is he married?" Elly asked.

"I don't think so."

Mulder went ahead, keeping himself between the women and the driver as he spoke. Scully blessed him for that.

"He's a nice boy," Elly said, using her chin to point at Mulder.

"Yes. I know."

In the middle of the street, Elly stopped, her lower lip trembling. "Is he right about this goblin?"

She nodded.

"I'm not ready to die yet, you know."

Dana squeezed the woman's arm. "I know. And you won't."

"Too mean, too cranky."

Dana smiled, although the woman didn't see her. "Well . . . I don't think so." She urged them forward again. "You're just tough, that's all. A good thing to be."

"Are you?"

Scully didn't know how to answer that one, and was saved from stumbling by Todd Hawks's arrival. It didn't take long to get Elly camped in her apartment, and not much longer than that, once they were outside again, to tell the chief they suspected that someone attached to, or working for, the Special Projects Office at Fort Dix was responsible for the murders. Someone, she added, who was extremely skilled at blending in.

"Disguises, you mean?" Hawks asked.

"You could say that."

"A real expert, one of the best," Mulder said, following her lead. Then he smiled so quickly she almost missed it. "You could say it gives a whole new meaning to the word wallflower."

"Son of a bitch." Hawks checked the sky as if daring the rain to add to his misery. "Damn, I don't need this. I really don't." He shook his head and looked up at Elly's apartment. The curtains were open; a lamp burned in the window. "If you don't mind telling me, you got anyone in mind?"

He sounded neither bitter nor imposed upon; he only sounded as if he wanted this to be over, so his town could get back to what passed for normal.

"Because," he added flatly, "what I've got is three goddamn corpses, and three families and some local politicians on my ass demanding explanations." He looked at Mulder then, eyes narrowed. "And would you happen to know why, while I was poking around Vincent's house this morning, a United States senator called my office?"

Oh, great, she thought; just great.

Though she could hear traffic in the distance, the neighborhood was quiet. A few lights on porches, in front windows; an old black dog trotting along the gutter; a large crow strutting across the ball field.

Like her, it seemed in a state of anticipation.

"Chief, can you patch Mulder through on your radio, to try to locate the rest of our team?"

"No problem," he said with a wry smile. "They were on their way to the station when I left, trying to find you."

When Mulder questioned her with a look, she shook her head slightly, waiting until Hawks was on the radio. "We've been sloppy," she said, matter of fact, not a scolding. "The major's ready to bolt, and all we've been able to do is run from one killing to another."

"The restaurant," he suggested.

She frowned. "Why?"

"Hank does his best thinking in front of a plate of pancakes."

"Mulder," she started, then waved herself silent. "Okay."

Then she hurried inside to be sure Elly was all right, a concern quickly allayed when she saw Spike on the stool, cap in his lap, avidly listening to the old woman describing her lifelong hunt for goblins.

Neither noticed her in the doorway; neither noticed when she left.

Hank was at the curb when she reached the sidewalk, Mulder already in the car, waving her around the back to the other door. The chief stopped her at the rear bumper.

"You'll let me know what I need to know?"

She promised, then swore when her shoulder bag slipped off and hit the ground. I have got to get control, she snapped at herself, and was grateful when Hawks crouched down to help her fetch her things. She had to kneel to grab a pen that had rolled beneath the car, only half-listening as Hawks made some lame jokes about a woman's purse.

She leaned over, saw the pen, and reached for it.

And froze.

"You need help?"

She shook her head and backed out, the pen retrieved and in her pocket. Then, as he helped her to her feet, something about the license plate puzzled her, froze her again until she saw it.

"Listen, Agent Scully, if there's something the matter—"

"No." She waved off his offered hand. "No, thank you, I'm fine. I just thought of something, that's all." She knew he didn't really believe her, but didn't know the right question to ask. "Thanks," she said, and slipped into the car.

As soon as she was settled, Andrews turned around to ask what next. As far as she was concerned, all they were doing was chasing their own tails, and widened her eyes when Scully said, "Exactly. That's why we're going to the restaurant, order a long lunch, and get things straight before we start tripping over ourselves."

"And what about our goblin?" Mulder asked quietly.

"Our goblin," she said, "won't be out again until tonight."

TWENTY-ONE

Despite the day's gloom, the Queen's Inn's lights were kept low, giving the room an evening feel. Two diners sat at the counter, each reading a newspaper; a family of six sat in the last booth, one of the children describing the movie he had seen on TV that morning, complete with explosive sound effects and dialogue quotations. A busboy swept the already gleaming floor. In the parking lot, a trailer truck took its time making a wide U-turn, causing a minor backup and a brief flurry of angry horns.

"Another peaceful day in the country," Mulder said glumly. He sat by the window, pushed into the corner, his topcoat draped over the seatback. Although his head no longer throbbed to distraction, his side refused to give him respite. He squirmed, thought he was settled, and then a quick stitch made him shift again.

The others didn't seem to notice his discomfort.

Hank sat across from him, gleefully, for Scully's benefit, attacking a steak with all the trimmings he'd been able to think of, while Andrews and Scully settled on salads. All he could think of was pancakes and bacon, so forced himself to order just a sandwich. Two seconds later, he had forgotten what kind it was.

The truck finished its turn.

The kid finished the movie to the laughing applause of his family.

Mulder shifted again. "Do you know what W. C. Fields said about children?"

Licia asked him who W. C. Fields was.

"I'm not old, you know," he said to Scully's infuriatingly blank expression. "Really. I am not old."

"Eat, Mulder," she ordered. "We have to work to do."

There was, then, mostly silence as they finished their meal. And once the table had been cleared, Scully flipped over her paper place mat and pulled out her pen, and looked to Mulder, who nodded it was her show, be my guest.

The family left.

The men at the counter paid and left as well.

"Pierce," Scully said, lightly jabbing the place mat with her pen, "was killed on a Saturday night. So was Corporal Ulman. Almost a pattern until last night." She paused, and Mulder was grateful she didn't mention Carl's name. "It's my guess Dr. Tymons is dead, too. Probably sometime yesterday." She filled them in quickly on what they had seen at Walson after the others had left, but gave neither of them a chance to comment. "The Project, whatever it is, is over."

"For now," Mulder added.

"All right. For now. And we don't have much time." She tapped the place mat again. "All the deaths are the same—throat slashed, deeply. This isn't a professional's attack. The violence . . . and the fact that each one came from the front, not behind . . ." She took a breath and shook her head. "It's almost psychotic. And the strength to do this indicates it's probably a man. Or," she added, when Mulder opened his mouth to comment, "a woman, okay. These days, there are a lot of women who go for weight training, defense training, things like that. We can't rule that out."

"Which means," Andrews said sourly, "we've narrowed it down to about eight or nine thousand people, right?"

"Wrong."

Mulder sat up, staring at the doodles Scully had drawn on the paper.

"While Pierce may have died just because he was in the wrong place at the wrong time, it's pretty obvious the others are connected. The corporal worked for Major Tonero—although we can't guarantee he knew everything that was going on, Carl Barelli was asking questions about goblins, and Dr. Tymons was the Project head."

She scribbled Tonero's name and circled it.

"I also think Mulder's right—the Project's in danger, and the goblin is cleaning house. Which is why we have someone staying with Ms. Lang." She circled Rosemary Elkhart's name. "That gives us motive. Hide the mistakes, bury the evidence. Literally."

"But if Tymons really is dead," Webber said, "won't that kill the project for good?"

"Oh, no. Not by a long shot. Dr. Elkhart, no matter what the major thinks, is in charge now. Nothing we said in that office fazed her, while the major was only partly acting. So I'm assuming she's gotten hold of the records, and I don't doubt she'd be able to have another center up and running before very long."

Andrews leaned forward eagerly. "She could have been planning it, you know. For weeks. Months, even. Something about the project, maybe it's almost ready, you know? I mean, done. Maybe she wants all the glory."

Scully tapped the name again. "I don't think there's any maybe about it, Licia."

"Then she did it!" Webber exclaimed.

Mulder blinked. "What? You think she's the goblin?"

Webber nodded, then shook his head, then threw up his hands. "Seemed like a good idea at the time." He brightened. "But she could be directing it. I mean, wouldn't she know who was a threat and who wasn't?"

Scully smiled. "Weekend nights," she reminded them. "Only weekend nights."

"So what are you saying?" Andrews asked with a frown. "We narrow it down to only those people who are free on weekends?" She shook her head. "Give me a break, okay?" She reached out to push at the place mat. "Do you know how many troops there are at Dix, for one thing? And every one of them—"

"Damn!" Mulder said.

Scully jumped, and he apologized with a quick gesture, but he had followed her road, marked the signposts, and the more he thought about it, the more he realized he already had the answer.

"What?" Webber said anxiously.

"Louisiana," he answered, speaking to Scully.

All she could do was look.

"That guy in Louisiana, he was supposed to have disappeared in the middle of a circus ring. Walked through a crowd of people and didn't come out the other side. But he was still there, Scully. He just didn't look the same way."

"And how do you know that?"

His left arm rested along the back of the seat, forcing him to turn toward her. "You'll be happy to know that I don't think he just disappeared in a puff of sawdust. He had to be there;

he was just different, that's all. The police were looking for one thing, so they didn't see anything else."

"Okay, so things weren't what they seemed. What does that have to do with this?"

"Ghosts and goblins, Scully. Ghosts and goblins."

"Meaning?" Andrews said testily.

"Meaning our field of suspects has just been made considerably smaller."

Rosemary stood his pacing, his ranting, for as long as she could. Then she came around the desk and said, "Joseph."

He ignored her. "God damn them, anyway. Did you see the way they spoke to me? Who the hell do they think they are?"

"Joseph."

He shook his head in exasperation. "This is too much. It's just too much." His face reddened, and he aimed a kick at one of the cartons. "And I even packed my damn keys away! Jesus H. Rosie, the whole world's gone nuts!"

She leaned back against the desk.

"Son of a bitch bastards are not—I repeat, are not—going to get away with it. I'll call that god-damn senator myself and—"

"Joseph!"

He whirled on her, one fist up, but she didn't flinch. She only softened her expression, and beckoned with a crooked finger. "Joseph." Her voice deep in her throat. "Joseph."

His chest rose and fell, the fist trembled and fell away.

"Joseph, there's nothing to worry about."

"What? How the hell—"

"Nothing to worry about," she repeated calmly, and beckoned him again.

This time he moved, close enough for her to place a hand on his shoulder.

"Everything we need from downstairs we already have. Everything we need from here is ready to ship."

"Yes, but—"

She hushed him with a finger on his lips. "And everything you need is right here, too."

She kissed him softly, quickly, and used all her remaining control to stop herself from slapping him.

"You have the orders?"

He leaned around her and yanked open the center drawer, pulled out a folder and handed it to her. "Signed and sealed, Rosie."

"Good." She pressed the folder against her chest. "Now we can either forget about downstairs altogether, because no one will see it for weeks, maybe even months. Or we can get Captain Whatshisname from Battalion to clean it up." She smiled. "After all, what are soldiers for?"

"I say we just leave it." The flush had receded from his cheeks and brow. He puffed a little, slipping back into his role. "And I say we don't wait for tomorrow morning."

"I don't mind."

"I can get us a flight tonight."

She considered it, and nodded. "Not too late, though. I want to get there in time to get a decent night's sleep."

His expression made her shudder. "Who says we'll get any sleep?"

"I do, you dope." She slapped his shoulder playfully and slipped around him, heading for the door. "We sleep, we see the right people, you take that leave, and then . . . who knows?"

Tonero laughed. "Okay, Rosie, okay." Then he frowned. "But what about—"

"All taken care of, darling." She picked up her coat from the chair. "All it takes is one phone call."

She waved, showed him a little chest movement, and left before he could think of anything else. There was no doubt he would make all the proper arrangements; she trusted him that much. As for the actual flight itself . . . she never had minded traveling alone.

In Elly Lang's apartment, the telephone rang.

Mulder knew that Scully was about to tug on the reins, haul him in before his excitement got the best of him. Nevertheless, he couldn't help the way his hands moved, darting from the notes on the place mat to his uneaten sandwich to tracing diagrams in the air only he could see.

"Civilian, first." He made sure they were listening with a look and a gesture. "Dr. Elkhart has no influence over military personnel without Major Tonero. And Tonero isn't about to use the military for project experiments. If it blew up, he'd lose his ticket to whatever election he's hoping to win when he retires."

Hank gaped, astonished. "How—"

"Us, second." He touched Scully's shoulder to keep her attention, and looked at Andrews. "It wasn't magic that told the goblin where we were yesterday. It wasn't magic that told the goblin where Carl would be last night." He scratched through his hair, then slapped it impatiently back into place. "Somebody knows us. Somebody who knows where we are most, if not all, of the time."

"Damn," Hank said. "Somebody who even knows what the hell we had for breakfast!"

It was all Mulder could do to keep the young man from jumping out of his seat.

"Right," Scully said, her eyes slowly widening. "And she was supposed to have a date with him last night. It was in his notes." She slipped out of the booth and grabbed her shoulder bag. "We talk to her now. Before—"

"Absolutely," Mulder agreed. "But not for the reason you think."

"But it has to be," Andrews protested. "God, it all fits. She's alone, so she comes and goes whenever she wants and nobody to question her, she has that equipment to keep in shape—" She grabbed Webber's arm, to pull him from the booth. Her voice began to rise. "She—"

Scully silenced her with a harsh wave and stared at Mulder. "Well?"

He moved more slowly, wincing when his side stabbed him again, dragging his coat along behind him. "She's not going anywhere, Scully." He tilted his head toward the window. "It's still too light."

He urged the others ahead with a nod, then tugged on Scully's coat to keep her back.

"It's not her," he said, keeping his voice low.

"How can you know that?"

He shook his head—tell you later—and gestured to Webber to cover the back, Andrews to stay outside.

"I don't know," Scully said, following him into the office.

"Three against one?" He banged the counter bell. "Come on, that's a bit much, don't you think?"

"She's psychotic," she reminded him when he hit the bell again. "And she's strong, Mulder." Her hand slipped into her purse, and didn't come out.

Mulder struck the bell once more, then rounded the counter and pushed through the beaded curtain. "Mrs. Radnor?" A staircase immediately to his left was dark. From the room at the back he heard muffled music, and hurried down the short hall.

"Mrs. Radnor!"

He stepped into the room, where the motel owner pumped furiously on a stationary bike, headphones on, listening to music from a cassette player lashed to the handlebars. She started when she saw him, her eyes wide and mouth open when she saw Scully, and the drawn gun.

"What the hell?" She held up one hand while the other very slowly pulled the headphones off and switched off the player. "Mr. Mulder, what's going on?"

"You don't seem terribly broken up about Carl Barelli," Scully said, keeping the gun at her side.

Mrs. Radnor tried to speak and couldn't; she could only look at Mulder for help, and an explanation.

He grabbed the handlebars and leaned toward her. "Mrs. Radnor, I haven't got time to explain, but I need to know something."

"Hey, I run a clean place here," she said. "You can't—"

"Frankie Ulman."

"I—what about him?"

"You told Agent Andrews you saw the corporal bring a date here every so often."

The woman nodded, her hands shifting to grip the towel draped around her neck.

"You told her you didn't know who the woman was."

"Well . . . yes."

"Why?"

"I didn't have time, for one thing." She forced a laugh. "She was in such a hurry, I don't think we talked more than five or ten minutes."

Mulder frowned, but shook it off. "You lied, Mrs. Radnor," he said carefully, and shook the bike slightly when she started to protest. "You knew who it was. You know just about everyone around here, and you knew who it was."

She moped her face, a stalling tactic, until Scully cleared her throat and made sure she remembered the gun. "I don't want to get people in trouble, you know? It's bad for business. Word gets around and—"

"Mrs. Radnor," he snapped, "we don't have time for this, okay? I'm only going to ask you once: Who was that woman?"

When she told him, he whirled. "Scully, get the car and Webber." He turned back as Scully charged from the room. "Mrs. Radnor, I have a favor to ask."

"What?" She couldn't believe it.

He smiled, and she softened almost immediately. "I need to borrow your car."

"What?" This time she almost yelled.

Jesus, woman, he thought, would you please stop—

"Commandeer," he said quickly. "I must commandeer your car."

Her face brightened. "Wow. You mean, like in the movies."

"Exactly." He took her arm and pulled her gently from the bike. "Just like the movies."

"But you had two—"

"The other one was shot up. But you know that already, right?"

Excited, flustered, she fumbled in her purse, held out the keys, and snapped them back. "Is this one going to get shot up?"

"I sincerely hope not," he said truthfully, took the keys from her hand before she could change her mind, and ran.

"But what if it is?" she yelled after him.

"The President will buy you a new one!" he yelled back, slammed through the front door, and grabbed the edge to swing him back inside.

"Pink," Mrs. Radnor called. "It's the pink Caddy in back."

Pink, he thought as he ran out again; terrific.

And thought *terrific* again when the storm finally broke, and broke hard.

TWENTY-TWO

"Vincent?" Scully gripped the dashboard as Mulder squealed out of the parking lot. The Caddy took a second to grip the slick tarmac and soon lost the Royal Baron in a swirling, twisting mist. "Officer Maddy Vincent?"

Webber and Andrews followed behind, their car nothing more than a smear of headlights.

Despite the storm, Mulder didn't bother to check his speed. Either what traffic there was got out of his way, or it didn't, it was their choice. He had a difficult enough time seeing through the rain.

"It's why Carl wanted to talk to her," he explained. "He wanted what he thought she knew about who was what, where, at the time of the killings." He grunted as the car threatened to fishtail. "Who else knows where all the cops will be, Scully? Who else knew where we would be yesterday?"

"Mulder, that's not enough."

He knew that. "Watch your back."

"Huh?"

"The goblin said 'Watch your back' to me, out there in the woods. Just before I was clobbered. This morning, on the way back from Tonero's, Vincent told Spike to watch his back." He glanced at her. "The same voice, Scully. It was the same voice."

He plowed through a lane-wide puddle, sending a wave soaring over the shoulder onto someone's front lawn.

Ahead, a pickup doused the windshield with backspray, and he cursed as he set the wipers to their highest speed.

It was almost enough.

At the corner of his vision he saw her shift so she could watch him and the road at the same time. "The makeup," she said, recognition hitting home. "The calamine lotion. It's—"

He listened to her mumble to herself, then catch her breath as he pressed on the horn and rocketed past the truck.

She had caught it now; she had caught the scent.

"It's breaking down." She was thinking aloud. "Whatever treatment they were giving her is breaking down. If . . . if it works correctly, she ought to be able to revert to normal color with no residual effects. It isn't happening. Mulder, it isn't happening, and she has to hide it somehow."

He had no argument.

The Project had failed; he guessed it wasn't the first time. He also suspected that Elkhart and Tymons had come closer than they ever had before, which was why the doctor and the major were packing to leave.

They were going to try again.

And he still couldn't shake the image of shadow armies, sliding through the night.

Another car ahead, its taillights flaring red as the driver pumped his brakes. Mulder grunted and swerved quickly into the other lane without reducing speed, and frantically spun the wheel right when the blinding bright headlights of an oncoming van blurred across the windshield.

It was too late to slow down.

He swung around the leading car on its right, fighting the wheels' stubborn inclination to take them straight into the woods, ignoring the frightened, angry blare of the other car's horn. His side began to burn. The Caddy jounced through a pothole, and he was on the road again.

"Mulder," Scully said calmly, "we can't help anyone if we're dead."

He stared at her in near panic. "Jesus!" He slapped the wheel with a palm. "Elly! If she's cleaning up . . . Elly!"

"But how?"

"Vincent's the dispatcher. All she has to do is call—who cares with what excuse?—and Spike is gone on some fool's errand. And Elly is alone."

He swung to the shoulder and braked, was out with the engine still running, instantly drenched and waving his arms. The car he had just passed swept by and honked loud and long as it emptied a puddle onto his legs. But Webber saw him and pulled up, Andrews rolling down her window before the car had fully stopped.

Mulder grabbed the door and leaned in. "Get to the station Hank. Find out where Vincent is, go there, and wait."

"Vincent?" Webber said incredulously. "You're kidding. Vincent?"

"Just do it, Hank," he ordered. He turned, and turned back. "And be careful. If Scully's right and she's gone off because something's gone wrong, she definitely won't hesitate to cut a couple of FBI throats."

There was no time for details. He jumped back into the Caddy and pushed the accelerator all the way down. The rear wheels spun, kicking pebbles and mud before they found traction and leap onto the blacktop again.

Webber's car had already vanished into the rain.

Elly Lang jumped when a gust of wind rattled the bay window. But she wouldn't panic. She had her spray can, she had the cane with the large ivory knob Officer Silber had found in her bedroom closet, and she had his promise he would be back in less than ten minutes.

Still, she was frightened.

The storm had come so suddenly, after so long a wait, and the light had dimmed so fast, that it was hard to believe it was only a few minutes past noon.

It wasn't, she told herself; not really.

It was midnight.

Time for the goblins to make their rounds.

Shadows snaked down the wall behind her, over her, while the rush of water in the eaves sounded too much like thunder.

She had been told to leave the lamp on, but soon after Silver left, she had turned it off. It was better this way. She could see outside better, and she hoped it would be harder for someone to see in.

The window rattled again.

The rain fell harder, and pellets of hail shotgunned against the panes.

I'm ready, she thought; I'm ready.

And then she wondered if she had locked the back door.

Rosemary Elkhart stood in the middle of her living room and decided it was hopeless. She hadn't been here five minutes, had barely taken off her coat, when Joseph had called, demanding reassurance that he wouldn't be burned, that his reputation would be intact, that no one would find Tymons's body in the woods. She had done her best, but second thoughts changed her mind after his third call.

He was hopeless.

After all this time, after all the bases and posts and installations they had been on, working through the kinks and dead ends of Leonard's discovery, Major Tonero had become, virtually on the night of their success, hopeless.

And a hell of a pain in the ass.

Worse; she had been around him long enough to know what that meant—cut your losses, cover your ass, offer the sacrifice, and start again somewhere else.

With someone else.

She looked with regret at the suitcases waiting near the door. To give him his due, he had bought her a lot of nice things, jewelry and clothes, some of which she had begun to convert to cash as soon as it became apparent that this phase of the project, while not perfect, was nearing its end.

A girl, she thought, can't be too careful.

Cover your ass.

Cut your losses.

And something else:

Travel light.

She picked up the bag at her feet, made sure

Leonard's disks were inside, then zipped it closed and reached for her coat. A cab to Philly would be expensive, but she considered it an investment. God knows there were plenty of private businesses out there, not necessarily in this country, who would be more than willing to learn what she knew.

She checked the bag again, recognizing her nervousness, and reminded herself that somehow, between here and the airport, she'd have to lose the gun.

"Okay," she said, and smiled at the room. "Okay."

At the moment she didn't give a damn for Madeline Vincent. The woman would have to learn to fend for herself. For what little time she had left.

She hadn't taken two steps when someone knocked on the door.

Mulder swore and slapped the steering wheel angrily when storm-slowed traffic finally forced his speed down.

Dana didn't scold. She had been infected by his urgency as well, to the extent that she lowered her window and tried to see if there was a way he could pass again on the right. Parked cars lined the curbs, however, for as far as she could see, and she didn't see suggesting he use the sidewalk as a lane.

If she did, he'd do it.

"Two blocks," she told him. "Just two blocks."

Equally frustrating was the lack of communication between here and the others. If she had a radio, she could have called ahead to Hawks and double-checked on Webber, and on Silber's being at the apartment.

She sighed and opened her bag, to be sure her weapon was loaded and ready.

Her hand touched something else.

Oh God, she thought, and debated for nearly a full minute before making up her mind.

The drum of rain on the roof forced her to raise her voice: "Mulder—"

"I wish I could fly," he said, glaring at the windshield as if that would give his vision a better chance. As it was, the rain was so hard, with the wind blowing now, that it seemed as if the street had been invaded by drifting fog.

"Mulder, listen."

He nodded. "Okay. Sorry."

"The shooter."

"What? Now?" He shook his head, and raised his hand to use the horn, changed his mind and throttled the steering wheel instead.

"Yes. Now." She tossed a sprig of pine onto the dashboard, and waited for him to see it. When he looked, she said, "It was caught under the car. Hank's car. I found it when we were at Elly's."

He was bewildered and lifted a shoulder. "So?"

"So Mrs. Radnor only spoke with Licia for five or ten minutes. So Licia has been fighting you every inch of this investigation. So Hank and I are the only ones who have used that car, and I know damn well I didn't hit or run over any tree." She stopped. Looked outside. "Hawks said they found the spot where the shooter had backed off the road into the woods. It wasn't a clear area." Her hands danced an apology over her lap. "I didn't read her notes, Mulder. She said she had them, I even watched her put them in her brief-case . . . but I didn't read them. And she didn't bring them to your room."

"Scully—"

"I screwed up." Her hands again. "Damnit, I screwed up."

"Nope," he said, rocking back and forth, body English for the car. "If I was dead, then you would have screwed up." She saw the grin. "Then I'd have to haunt you."

"Mulder, that's not funny."

"But you don't believe in ghosts and goblins."

Hail bounced off the hood.

She jumped when a car honked behind them.

"So," he said, "what do we do?"

"We take care of business," she said without hesitation. "And when that's done, we take care of more business."

He nodded, groaned when traffic came to a complete halt, and finally unsnapped his seat belt. "Take the car."

She reached out to grab his arm, but she was too late. "Mulder!"

He stood in the middle of the street, rain dripping into his eyes. He pointed. "I can't wait, Scully. I can't. Just . . ." He flapped the hand helplessly. "Just come after me as fast as you can."

He was gone, the cars behind discovered their horns, and she slid awkwardly into the driver's seat, all the while watching him race to the sidewalk and around the next corner.

If there were any rules left in the book that he hadn't broken, she couldn't think of them.

All she could think of was, watch your back, Mulder. For God's sake, watch your back.

TWENTY-THREE

He knew he must have looked like a fool, racing headlong through the rain, one hand held loosely over his head in feeble protection against the hail that, so far, was no larger than a pea. That didn't stop it from stinging, however, and stinging badly.

He bolted across the street, veering sharply when a minivan nearly clipped him on his blind side. He skidded, fell into a parked car, and used it to propel him onto the sidewalk again.

The hail stopped.

The rain didn't.

He didn't want to, but he had to slow up—his side had begun to pull, and he couldn't help thinking that something had torn in there.

Hang on, Elly, he thought; hang on.

At the next intersection, he paused under a tree, half bent over, hands hard on his hips, and took precious seconds to get his bearings, and his breath back. Another block west, he thought, swallowed hard, and tried to run, snarling when he couldn't do much better than a fast trot.

A winter-raised section of concrete made him swerve onto a lawn, where he slid on the wet grass and went down on his hands and knees. It felt good, not moving, and it took him a moment to get back on his feet.

He had no choice but to run now, forcing the pain in his side to another place, one that didn't bother him, one he knew would exact a great price when he couldn't concentrate any longer.

The wind pushed a curtain of water into his eyes. He slapped it away angrily without missing a step as he charged off the curb and across the tarmac to the other side. He figured Scully, with her luck, would beat him there anyway, but at least now he was moving, doing something instead of cursing traffic and feeling helpless.

Reaching the next corner seemed to take hours, and when he stopped, he almost panicked.

This wasn't right; he was on the wrong street.

Strings of mist like ghosts moved slowly through the rain; a storm drain overflowed, creating a shallow pond across the intersection.

This wasn't right, and he didn't know which way to go.

Then he saw the park across the way and up the block, the benches and ball field obscured by the rain. His lips parted—it wasn't quite a grin—and he moved on, his face turned toward the houses he passed to keep his vision clear.

The police car was gone.

The lamp was out in Elly's window.

He slowed as he approached the front walk, slipping his left hand into his pocket to wrap around his gun. Front or back? Wait for Scully, or do the stupid thing and go in on his own?

He had no realistic alternative.

He reached the front walk just as a horn honked several times in quick succession. Turning as he ran, he saw Scully bump the pink Cadillac up over the curb and practically throw herself into the street.

Sometimes you just live right, he thought, and waved her around to the back, ran up the steps and stopped with his hand on the knob.

The wind shrieked overhead.

Something rattled down a drainpipe.

He fought his lungs into calming, then stepped into the foyer. Slowly now, knowing he wouldn't be able to give Scully enough time, he sidled to the door and put an ear to the damp wood.

Nothing; the storm made it impossible to hear a thing.

He tried the knob, and closed his eyes briefly when it turned, mouthed a *damn*, and turned it, using his shoulder to push the door inward.

The living room was dark, and empty, grey light from the bay window the only illumination. Rain shadows rippled across the furniture and carpet. An ivory-topped cane lay on the floor in front of the couch.

He could see no light in the kitchen, or in the bedroom at the front room's far side.

He chose the kitchen first.

Keeping as close to the wall as he could, he moved down the short hall. As far as he could see, no one sat at the little table, and he could see no welcome, telltale shadow in the back door window.

Water slipped from his hair and down his spine.

A shudder briefly hunched his shoulders.

Closer, gun aimed toward the ceiling, and he braced himself, counted to three, and stepped quickly into the kitchen, sweeping the barrel ahead of him.

No one was there.

He eased back toward the living room, heard a scraping, and spun around as Scully came through the back door, a sharp shake of her head letting him know there was no one outside, and no sign of Elly.

Or the goblin.

No words, then. Hand signals told her they must be in the bedroom. She nodded, once, and he took the hall again, shoulders brushing along the wallpaper.

Listening, and hearing only the wind, only the rain.

When he sensed Scully directly behind him, he stepped in and crossed the floor in four long strides. The bedroom door was open, but it was too dark for him to see much more than the shadowed outline of a brass headboard.

Time, he thought; *no time.*

Scully positioned herself opposite him at the door, and at her nod, they went in, he high, she low.

"Damn." He kicked at the bed.

The room was empty.

They were too late; Elly Lang was gone.

Rosemary adjusted the bag's strap over her shoulder, smoothed the lapels of her coat, and shook her head.

"You're an idiot, Joseph," she said, opened the door, and left.

"Maybe she's hiding," Scully said.

Mulder doubted it, but together they took less than five minutes looking into every place large enough to hold a woman Elly's size, not at all surprised when all they found was dust and cans of orange spray paint.

He stood in the middle of the living room, absently tapping the gun against his leg.

"Think," he told himself. "Think!" When Scully rejoined him, he shook his head. "She either left on her own, or she's been taken. And I don't think she—"

The front door slammed open, and they instantly dropped into defensive crouches, their guns aimed and ready to fire.

"Hey, no!" Webber cried, throwing up his hands. "Jeez, guys, it's me!"

"Hank," Mulder said, ready to strangle him. He straightened stiffly and lowered his weapon. "You are an idiot. Don't you know better than that?"

Webber tried to point in several directions at once. "I'm sorry. I saw the car, and the outside door was open, and I thought . . ." He paled. "Jesus. Oh, Jesus." Without looking at either of them, he dropped into the chair and leaned over, hands dangling between his legs. "I could have been killed, you know that? I'm so stupid, I could have been killed."

Scully offered him no sympathy. She stood in front of him, and poked his foot with her shoe. "Where's Andrews?"

"What?" He looked up, confused. "What are you talking about? She was right—"

"Here," Andrews said, standing in the door-way. Her gun was out, and it was aimed at Mulder's head. "Right here."

• • •

"How much do you charge to go to the airport?" Rosemary asked the cabbie.

"Which one?"

"Philadelphia."

"Lady, are you kidding? In this weather?"

"Whatever it is," she said, holding up her purse, "I'll double it. For the trip over. And for your trip back."

He shook his head doubtfully. "Lady, I don't know. They're saying there's flash floods—"

She took out her gun. "You either make money, or you die." She smiled. "Your choice."

Andrews shifted to her right so she could still keep Mulder in her sights while keeping the wall at her right shoulder.

He held his empty hands wide at his sides. "You're not doing an awful lot of thinking."

She shrugged. She didn't much care. "Do I have to?" She shrugged again. "You're going to die, what's there to think about?"

"One against three is pretty awful odds," Scully said.

"Oh, God," Webber moaned. "I'm gonna be sick."

"Oh, shut up," Andrews snapped. "Christ, how the hell did you ever get in the Bureau?"

Mulder's gun was on the coffee table with Scully's, and all a leap for it would get him would be a bullet in the side, or in the head. Scully, who had been ordered to sit on the couch, was in no better position.

"Look," he said, "Elly is out there somewhere, with the goblin."

Webber sagged forward, one arm across his stomach. He sounded terrified. "Oh Christ." He retched dryly.

"What do I care about an old lady?" Andrews said. "And if you think you're going to stall me long enough for the cavalry to come, forget it. I watch movies, too, Mulder. I'm not as stupid as you think."

He denied any such idea with a shake of his head, and wished Webber would stop that infernal groaning. He couldn't hear himself think, and it was only making Andrews angrier than she already was. Then he snapped his fingers, making Scully jump and Andrews steady her gun hand. "Douglas." He frowned. "You work for Douglas?" His expression hardened. "Of course you do. Because you're not Bureau at all. Which makes me wonder who the mighty Douglas really works for?"

"Time's up," she said blandly.

"Oh, God," Webber gasped and slipped off the chair and onto one knee. "Oh, God, I'm gonna die."

With a look, Andrews dared Scully to make a move, then swung the gun back to Mulder, and smiled him a farewell.

He threw himself backward just before he

heard the shot, bracing himself for the impact, landing on his back and rolling to his left when he didn't feel a thing.

He heard Andrews cry out, though, and heard her fall, her gun clattering across the hall floor.

"Nice dive," Scully told him. She was on the floor by the table, her hand around her gun.

Webber pushed himself back into the chair and closed his eyes, his gun hand dangling over the armrest. "I almost missed her," he said to the ceiling. "Christ, can you believe it? I almost missed her."

Mulder jumped to his feet, angry and relieved at the same time. But he said nothing. He picked up his weapon, tucked it into his pocket, and stood over the fallen Andrews. Webber hadn't missed; the entry wound was through her right eye.

He pointed. "You will answer questions later, Hank. Right now, you stay with her. And I mean stay with her."

He didn't argue. His face was pale, his lips trembling; the only sign that he heard was a weak flutter of his hand.

Then Scully looked out the window and said, "Mulder, the park," and he was out the door at a run, taking the three steps at a leap.

She was there, on her bench, huddled beneath her umbrella, and probably had been there the whole time. He had been so intent on getting into the apartment, he hadn't bothered with a single glance across the street once he reached the building.

"Elly, are you all right?"

He slowed when he reached the sidewalk, walked when he started across the grass.

The woman nodded, but the umbrella was loose in her grip, and it nearly fell.

"It's okay, Elly," he said when he reached the bench. He leaned down and brushed a hand over her knee, then held up a hand to shade his eyes from the rain while he looked over the muddy field to the trees on the other side.

She could be there, he thought; damn, she could be anywhere.

"Mulder," the goblin said. "I thought I told you to watch your back."

TWENTY-FOUR

With a silent sigh he stared at the ground, at raindrops splashing out of the grass. Then he looked over his shoulder as he turned without haste, blinking the rain out of his eyes.

The umbrella had been discarded.

She sat on the bench back, wearing a long black coat that reached halfway down her shins, her bare feet on the seat, braced to spring. Her short dark hair was matted into a skullcap, her large dark eyes slightly crinkled, as if she were smiling.

Her left hand lay on her thigh, fingers drumming out of rhythm; her right hand held a bayonet, and he could see the gleam of the sharpened edge as she tapped it against her knee.

It was odd, this meeting. Like two friends coming across each other on a rainy day in the park. Only, one of them, before it ended, was going to die.

She raised an eyebrow. "I don't think so, Mulder. Not me, anyway."

"You can read minds, too?"

"No. But you have that gun in your coat, and I have—" She held up the bayonet. "It's not hard to figure out."

The water had taken most of her makeup off, and had washed the white lotion from the backs of her hands. The skin was mottled as if it were dying and ready to slough away in the rain, but it wasn't just gray and black. He could see blotches of pale green, dark green, and near her toes a smear of something almost red.

It could have been blood.

"Where's Elly?"

Maddy shrugged. "I don't know. I tried to get in the back door, and the next thing I knew I heard the front door slam." She laughed so hoarsely it made his throat ache. "I didn't know an old lady could run so damn fast. I would have gone after her, but as luck would have it, you showed up."

Her eyes shifted away, shifted back.

"Tell her to be careful, Mulder," Maddy suggested. "You may be fast, and a bullet is real fast, but it won't stop me from doing what I have to, understand?"

"I heard," Scully said from somewhere behind him.

He spread his arms. "It's silly, you know. I die, you die, it isn't going to do you any good."

Her voice deepened. "I'm already dying." She held out her hand. "It doesn't work anymore."

He couldn't believe it when her fingers *shifted*, flesh to splotchy green to smooth cream, and back. Except two of her knuckles stayed dark far longer.

She giggled. "What a bitch, huh? Instead of getting famous, I'm getting dead."

He didn't know what to say. Somehow, "You're under arrest for murder" sounded awfully stupid.

She giggled again, and that was when he saw the madness—in the tilt of her head, the movement of her eyes.

"Why?" he asked, gesturing at her skin. "Didn't you know how dangerous it was?"

"Sure." She waved the bayonet idly. "But do you know how much a cop in a burg like this makes? A dispatcher? Do you know how much that bitch gave me every month?" She laughed and rocked back, rocked forward quickly, bracing herself again. "She had pictures, I saw them, I can read, I knew the risk. Besides . . ." Her voice faded.

He waited, not moving when she began to toy with the coat's buttons, opening them, closing them, opening some and leaving them.

She wore no clothes beneath the coat, and that didn't surprise him. For what she could do, and had to do, clothes would have been a problem.

What he needed now was for Scully to get into position to cover him when he made his move. He had to. He couldn't stand here, waiting for her to decide it was time, and he wasn't about to let her go. No matter how sorry for her he felt. Which he did as she began to ramble about the tests in the room below the hospital, about the solution baths and the injections, about spying on her friends and on strangers and—

"—feeling such a sense of goddamn power, Mulder. Power." She grinned; her teeth were brown and black. She whispered, "Power."

"Maddy," he said, "don't do this."

"Oh, knock it off," she snapped, straightening, the bayonet catching silver light from the rain. "You can't appeal to my better nature. I don't have one anymore. You can't offer me a cure. You, and you," she shouted to Scully, "can't offer me a damn thing."

"How about living a while longer?"

She laughed, and brushed a strand of hair from her eyes. "Who's going to stop me, you? Her?"

"I can bet Elly's called the police by now. They take one look at you, they won't stop to talk."

"Big deal. I'll be gone." She bounced a little on her rump. "Don't you know I'm the Invisible Woman?"

Her eyes again, shifting, frowning. Scully had moved to his left and was moving to get behind her. One step at a time.

"She's not fast enough, you know."

He lifted his right hand. "Fast enough, if she has to be."

Maddy tensed.

He knew it was coming, and as soon as he recognized it, the calm finally returned.

The wind nudged her, and she hugged herself, then slipped off the coat.

He only just managed to keep his expression from reacting to the sight of her, skin rough in one place, seemingly raw in another, dark clouds of color rippling across the ridged plane of her stomach.

"You know something?" she said, licking her lips, gauging distance.

"What?" He kept his voice quiet and steady.

"I learned a lot from that bitch. I'm going to tell her that before she dies."

"Like what? What can you learn from killing people?"

She grinned. "That I like it."

He saw her toes flex.

"Please," he said, just before she giggled.
Just before she jumped.

There was no time to pull his gun from his pocket. He twisted away from the blade and, at the same time, fired through the coat, lost his footing in the slippery grass and fell on his back.

Maddy screamed when she landed on her hands and knees, spun around, and tried to stand.

"Stop!" Scully ordered, rushing up, aiming low.

Mulder couldn't stand, couldn't move; he could only watch as Maddy Vincent feinted with the blade, then tried to run–crawl at him.

"Stop!" Scully yelled.

Maddy toppled onto one shoulder as if someone had put a boot in her back, and screamed again, stabbed the ground, and slumped whimpering into the mud.

As Mulder pushed himself to his feet, as Scully braced herself behind the woman, he saw the blood seep out from under her arm.

It didn't look black at all.

It looked red, and it didn't stop.

He leaned over and took the bayonet from her hand, held it close to his eyes for a moment and placed it on the bench. Scully pressed three fingers to the side of the woman's neck, then checked her wrist. She rose awkwardly, a hand pushing through her hair, and Mulder took off his coat and spread it over the goblin's body.

He stared at it for a long while, until he laughed once, sharply, realizing he had been waiting for her, like the Invisible Man, to return to normal, now that the adventure was finally done.

But she didn't.

She just lay there.

Mulder didn't know how long it took to answer the questions, for Scully to make sure the body would be placed in the right hands for the proper examinations, for the cold to finally leave him, for him to finally feel dry.

But it was after eleven that night before he was able to sit in the Queen's Inn and stare at the plate of pancakes in front of Hank Webber.

"Please," Hank said. "Don't say it's amazing."

"It is, but I won't."

Scully was at the counter, ordering coffee and tea, and finding out just what the cook would make this late on Saturday night. Mulder waited until her back was turned, then lifted a finger to get Hank's attention.

"Protest not," he said. "Don't insult me with denials. But how many times have you called Douglas since we've arrived, to tell him how many times I didn't follow the book."

Webber almost choked, but he managed to hold up his fork and say, "Just once."

"What?"

He looked embarrassed. "I couldn't. I mean . . .

I like you. And I didn't see that you were doing anything really wrong."

Mulder grinned as he stretched his arm across the back of the seat. "Webber, I don't care—that's damn amazing." He looked out the window, but all he saw was the night and the rain. "You know that Douglas is probably a plant, don't ask me by whom, and he probably won't be there when we get back. You know you'll probably be transferred somewhere else once we get back and the paperwork is done."

"Sure. I figured. But hell, it was fun while it lasted."

Mulder laughed, a little sadly, because he knew poor old Hank probably wouldn't be with the Bureau for very long. "Fun" wasn't exactly the way to describe the way it worked.

"And by the way," he said, "in all the excitement . . . thanks."

Webber waved it away. "Not needed, Mulder. I was just doing what I had to, you know?"

And he blushed.

Scully slid in then, clucked at Webber's choice of a meal, and fussed with her napkin while she waited for her order. "You do realize, Mulder, don't you, that that was an incredibly lucky shot. By all rights, you should be dead."

He knew that. He had especially known that when he had seen the rent across the front of his coat.

The blade had come a lot closer than he'd thought; it had sliced clear through the cloth.

"Don't ever try that again."

"Believe me," he said. "I won't."

They ate, then, in companionable, weary silence, interrupted only by a phone call he took at the register. When he returned to the booth, he only said, "They found Tonero's body. Shot once. He was in Dr. Elkhart's apartment."

"And her?" Scully asked.

"Gone. Not a trace."

"They'll find her," Webber said confidently. "After this weekend, half the country'll be hunting for her. Don't sweat it, Mulder, the case is closed."

"I suppose," Mulder said. He looked out the window, through the rivulets of rain. "I suppose."

Scully touched his shoulder, light and quick. "Mulder, don't."

He didn't look. "Sure."

They both knew he was lying.

Because, he thought, looking through his dim reflection to the woodland just beyond, what if they don't find her.

What if, next year, or the year after, you're walking down the street or climbing your steps or standing on your porch or you're waiting for a bus, and an arm comes out of a wall or a tree or . . .

He stretched a finger toward the glass, watching its reflection stretch toward him.

. . . a simple pane of glass.

The lights flickered for a moment, and for a moment the reflection vanished.

GOBLINS

He rubbed his arm absently, watching the headlights of a car he couldn't see float past and disappear.

We'll never know they're out there—
Armies of living shadows.
Slipping through the night.

The Best in Science Fiction and Fantasy

Today . . .

WRATH OF GOD by Robert Gleason. An apocalyptic novel of a future America about to fall under the rule of a murderous savage. Only a small group of survivors are left to fight — but they are joined by powerful forces from history when they learn how to open a hole in time. Three legendary heroes answer the call to the ultimate battle: George S. Patton, Amelia Earhart, and Stonewall Jackson. Add to that lineup a killer dinosaur and you have the most sweeping battle since *THE STAND*.
Trade paperback, 0-06-105311-2 — $14.99

THE X-FILES™ by Charles L. Grant. America's hottest new TV series launches as a book series with FBI agents Mulder and Scully investigating the cases no one else will touch — the cases in the file marked X. There is one thing they know: The truth is out there.
0-06-105414-3 — $4.99

THE WORLD OF DARKNESS™: VAMPIRE— DARK PRINCE by Keith Herber. The groundbreaking White Wolf role-playing game Vampire: The Masquerade is now featured in a chilling dark fantasy novel of a man trying to control the Beast within.
0-06-105422-4 — $4.99

THE UNAUTHORIZED TREKKERS' GUIDE TO *THE NEXT GENERATION* AND *DEEP SPACE NINE* by James Van Hise. This two-in-one guidebook contains all the information on the shows, the characters, the creators, the stories behind the episodes, and the voyages that landed on the cutting room floor.
0-06-105417-8 — $5.99

HarperPrism
An Imprint of HarperPaperbacks